Other Books by T.J. Mindancer

The Tales of Emoria

Book 1: *Future Dreams*
Book 2: *Present Paths*
Book 3: *Past Echoes*
Book 4: *Fall Time*

Hekolatis' Promise

The Queen's Sister

Novella
Bountiful Glen

BLOOD HERO

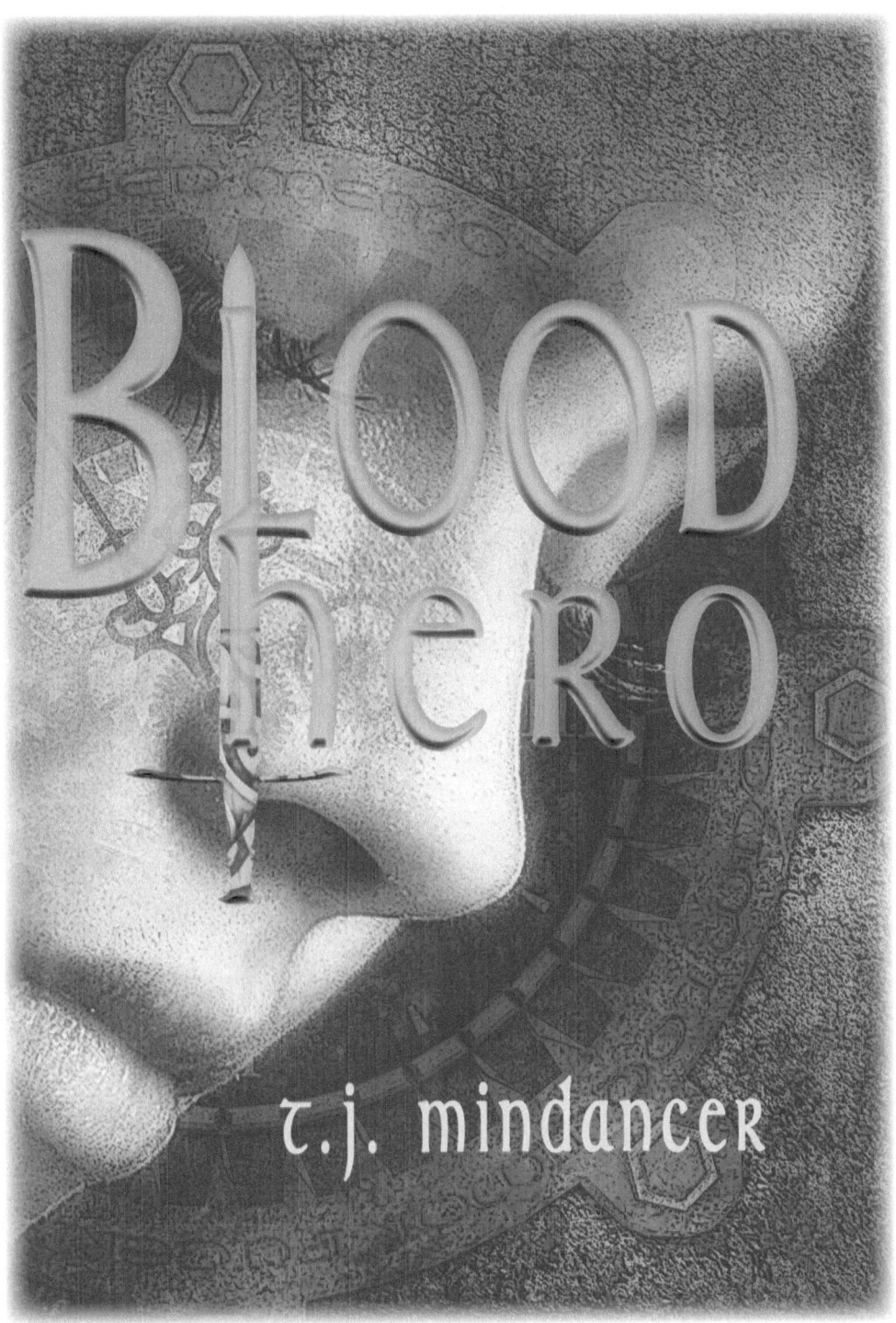

Blood hero

T.J. mindancer

Mindancer Press
Bedazzled Ink Publishing Company • Fairfield, California

978-0-9886061-7-3 paperback

Cover Design
by

Mindancer Press
a division of
Bedazzled Ink Publishing, LLC
Fairfield, California
http://www.bedazzledink.com

*For all those times I miss roaming around
the hills and hollows of the Shawnee National Forest.*

Part I
An Unusual Unsolvable Crime

Chapter 1

CHIEF CATHERINE "CUTTY" Cuthbertson-Downes lounged on the wood-plank bench in front of the Lipping Creek, Illinois police department and reveled in the warm autumn day. The wind was so calm the red and yellow leaves on the ancient oak sprawled on the circle green hung still, as if posing for the cameras of the endless stream of hikers, weekend nature lovers, and families who rolled through the two blocks of cheerful, renovated turn-of-the-twentieth-century storefronts.

Cutty always joked that her job was ninety-nine percent nothing to do punctuated by one percent of high drama—usually involving someone going off a bluff in White Bluffs State Park that pressed against the outskirts of town or rescuing lost or injured hikers or rock climbers in the surrounding national forest. The only thing that would make the day better would be the opportunity to hike the forest trails she loved.

The sun was overhead and knots of hikers, families, and bicyclists converged on Marge's Cafe next door as if Marge had rung the old firehouse bell that hung beside the half-glass door for lunch. Eating at Marge's was as much a part of the weekend at White Bluffs as exploring the park itself.

Patti, Marge's perky helper, squeezed through the growing line snaking out the cafe door. She saw Cutty and grinned as she trotted to her.

"Looks like the weather has brought out the fair-weather outdoor lovers." Sarah handed Cutty a small, bulging white bag.

"I don't think we could handle it if they were all-weather lovers." Cutty peeked inside the bag. The aroma of Marge's egg salad on thick slices of fresh-baked whole wheat bread reminded her that breakfast had been way too early that morning. "Smells like heaven. Tell Marge, thanks."

"Will do." Sarah shaded her eyes as she watched a stream of bicyclists spin onto the circle green at the top of the road. "The Tour de France just arrived. Better get back." She gave Cutty a wave as she trotted into the crowd. "Enjoy."

"You bet I will." Cutty pulled the fat sandwich from the bag. She unwrapped it, took a huge bite, and sat back happily chewing.

She looked over her little domain at its most crowded and, in a way, celebratory. How many places in the world could offer such simple pleasures that turned into the kind of day people looked back upon as magical? Especially days like today, that almost sparkled with autumn perfection.

She felt the joy emanating from the families at the picnic tables in front of the cafe and the hikers and bicyclists swapping directions and favorite spots to visit. They almost glowed with the radiant knowledge that they were a part of a special group who knew the best place to spend a gorgeous autumn Sunday.

And, best of all, she got to experience it with them.

"Thank you, Grandpa." She gazed at the street of houses that rose up on Downes hill behind the storefronts. Grandpa Downes lived in the white Victorian straight across from the police department. He now kept an eye on the domain he had overseen for forty years from his office in the turret of the house.

"Hey, Chief Cutty." A group of students from the university cycled by, waving at her.

She waved back. She got her last degree ten years ago, but her ties to the academic world were strong through her parents, who were professors at the university. She used to be a part of the biking club and was still an active member of the Audubon Society and Sierra Club. One foot remained firmly in academia, even as her heart roamed free beneath the canopy of the national forest.

She popped the last bite of her sandwich into her mouth. Time to get back to her desk and finish up the budget reports, which unfortunately didn't allow for extra help who would have let her take a beautiful weekend day off. She eased up off the bench and dropped the wadded bag into one of the concrete waste containers she had lobbied hard with the town council to get for Main Street.

Rapid movement caught the corner of her eye. Several people who looked like hard-core hikers rushed along the sidewalk across the street. They dodged around the unmoving lines of cars going both ways as they crossed the street.

Cutty could make the town a fortune on jaywalking tickets. Of course, she'd be issuing just as many tickets to herself and her own staff.

The hikers skirted around a couple trying to wrangle a brood of young ones toward Marge's and stopped in front of Cutty. They labored to catch their breaths. Their boots were freshly stained, and the odor of decaying leaves and vegetation clung to their Sierra Club chic clothes.

The wiry bespectacled man with thinning hair opened his mouth but could only suck in air.

"Take your time," Cutty said.

"Thank you," the man gasped as he finally got his breathing under control. "We just want to report something kind of strange."

"Okay. Why don't we step into the office?" Cutty opened the door and held it as the two men and two women shuffled in. "Have a seat on the bench. Do you need some water? We have some bottles in the fridge."

The hikers plopped down on the bench and gave her pathetically grateful looks.

"Yes, please," one of the women said.

Cutty went down the narrow corridor to the tiny kitchen and pulled five bottles of water from the fridge. She had to admit her curiosity was piqued. What kind of strange thing could they have come across in the forest?

She balanced the bottles in an awkward pyramid and walked back to the foyer. "Here ya go."

They each took a bottle from the balanced pile and drank down as much water as they needed while Cutty leaned against the service counter opposite the bench. She washed down the remnants of her sandwich with a few mouthfuls of water. "I'm Chief Cutty, by the way."

The wiry man nodded. "Rick. This is Jamie, Sarah, and Jason." He took a deep breath. "We were hiking down off of Gardner Ridge and were following the creek to look at the rock shelters."

Cutty nodded. "I know where you're talking about. There are petroglyphs in some of the shallow caves."

"Yes. We got photos for our next Sierra Club meeting." Rick took another sip of water. "Anyway. We were walking along and heard shouting."

"Muffled shouting," Jamie, a woman with ruddy cheeks and matching red hair, added.

"Muffled." Rick glanced at her and nodded. "We hurried to it and came to the mouth of a real cave."

Cutty frowned. "The only cave there is padlocked."

The hikers nodded and talked at once. They glanced at each other and gave Cutty sheepish looks then turned to Rick.

"Right," Rick said. "The shouting was coming from inside the cave. Not deep inside, but from someplace we couldn't see."

"Weird shouting." Jason pressed down his mustache with his fingers.

"A man was saying like, 'How did you get in here?' uh, 'Who are you?' and 'What do you want?' Stuff like that. He sounded shocked and surprised," Rick said.

"But the strangest thing was—" Jamie said.

"Oh, yeah. The strangest thing was a female voice. She said, 'I'm your destiny,' in an accent, like Irish or Scottish or something. And then the man started shouting, 'No no, no,' and then he gave a blood-curdling scream. I mean it sounded so close, he could have been right in front of us, but he wasn't." Rick exchanged haunted, wide-eyed glances with his companions. "Then it was quiet. Complete silence."

"Like eerie silence," Jamie said.

"We didn't know what to do, so we hid behind some trees to wait for someone to come out of the cave," Jason said. "But no one did. We were there for fifteen minutes, and we didn't see or hear anything else from the cave."

"The padlock was locked?" Cutty asked.

"Yes," they all said.

"Oh, and there was something else in the cave." Rick turned to the woman he had introduced as Sarah.

She pulled a professional-looking SLR camera from her backpack. She powered it on, clicked through the photos, and handed the camera to Cutty.

"This is inside the cave, through the bars in the door," Sarah said. "We can't see the wall on the right, but something metal is sticking out from behind the bulge hiding the wall."

Cutty lifted the camera closer to her eyes and studied the image on the oversized LCD display. Something long and grayish stood partially hidden.

"You can zoom with this." Sarah pointed to a button.

"Oh, thanks." Cutty pushed the zoom and centered the grayish object. "You guys saw it for real. What did it look like?"

The hikers exchanged glances.

"We thought it looked like a door," Rick said. "Like wide open, and all we saw was the outer edge."

Cutty studied the image. "That's what it looks like to me." She handed the camera back to Sarah. "Could I download this photo and any others you have of the cave?"

Sarah blinked at her. "Sure." She popped the memory card out of the camera and handed it to Cutty.

Cutty flashed her a smile. "Thanks."

She went around the service counter and pressed the memory card into a slot on the computer. She opened the disk file and created a new folder. She selected all the photos of the cave and moved them into the folder and sat back to wait for them to download.

Rick stood up. "There's one more thing." Jamie squeezed his arm for encouragement. "There was only one set of footprints in the cave. Going into the cave."

Cutty stared at their earnest faces. "One set?"

"I took photos of the cave floor, too." Sarah nodded at the computer.

Cutty nodded and put on her professional face, even as her mind raced around and screamed out her curiosity. "Well, thank you for reporting this."

The photos finished downloading and she gave the disk back to Sarah. She pulled business cards from a holder for each of them. "Just drop an email if you think of anything else."

"We will," Rick said.

The hikers pulled on their backpacks.

"I don't envy your job one bit," Jason said with a grin.

Cutty chuckled. "This is a bit more unusual than what I usually have to deal with. At least it makes my job more interesting. And you're right. This is a strange one, but hopefully it has a simple explanation. That cave is on a strip of private land that extends to the road."

"Private?" Jamie turned to the others, who looked panicked. "We didn't see any signs."

Cutty smiled. A lot of the Sierra Clubbers were almost obsessive about doing things by the book. "Some owners allow hikers to cross their property—especially the areas that hikers can't easily go around. The owners can't complain if they don't post signs."

The hikers looked beyond relieved.

"We would never knowingly trespass on private property," Rick said.

"That's good to hear," Cutty said.

A few minutes later, Cutty stood outside the door, waving goodbye to the hikers as they hurried back across the street. The crowd in front of Marge's was much thinner. A group of bicyclists rolled in off a side street and gathered on the patch of green around the flag and monument at the top of the block—the traditional gathering place for the two-wheelers.

She gazed at the white bluffs beyond the edge of town. Was this report really as strange as it sounded? Or were the owners of the property working in their cave and watching an action DVD or something.

She often wished something more exciting than rescuing hikers would happen. She took a deep breath. "Be careful what you wish for."

PAULA REISLING, DIRECTOR of the Repository of Unusual Unsolvable Crimes, took a long sip of coffee, pushed up her wire-rimmed glasses, and studied the contraption sprawled over a good quarter of Bay 3. The thing looked like a Rube Goldberg invention caught in a nonsensical Google search.

Jeff, Assistant Archivist, was crashed out on the older-than-dirt sofa. His red hair stuck out everywhere, the stubble on his cheek was now a beard, and he had on a worn Blue Devil Duke t-shirt and sweats of indeterminate color and age. His flip-flops were closer to being just flops with the tenuous hold of string and duct tape.

Paula walked around the mismatch of twisted metal, wires, cables, and serious-looking electronics. "Maybe we can sell it to the Museum of Modern Art."

She peered at an intertwined mess of red, green, yellow, and brown cables.

"Or it can be a diabolical test for the bomb squad."

Jeff pulled himself up and twisted around to sit properly on the sofa. He ran his hands over his face. "It made sense for about five minutes two days ago. Then I had to figure out what to do with all the extra stuff."

"Looks more like a weapon of mass confusion." Paula sighed and walked to the work table scattered with papers and notebooks filled with jittery script. She sorted through the messy piles until she found the case file folder.

Jeff stood up, pressed his fists into the small of his back, and stretched. "I don't know what the killer thought this was, but it's not even a good erector set project."

Paula read through the crime report for the millionth time. "Why would someone commit an unsolvable crime for no solvable reason?" She chuckled. Of course, that was why the case had been laid to rest in her repository.

"Well, it was worth a try," Jeff said.

"And this case seemed to have some promise." Paula put the folder on the table.

Jeff shrugged. "I guess we keep looking until we find one we can solve."

Paula took in his drooping eyes and slumped body. "You gave it a valiant try. Go sleep it off."

Jeff grinned. "Thanks, boss." He picked up his hoodie and shuffled out of the bay.

Paula leaned back against the work table and gazed at the Rube Goldberg nightmare. Were they nuts to challenge themselves to try to solve one of these unsolvable crimes? On the other hand, it broke up the monotony of organizing and cataloging a building full of evidence from hundreds of nefarious goings-on. And they got to use their collective degrees in history, criminology, anthropology, mechanical engineering, and, of course, the necessary archives.

She straightened and paced around the cavernous bay. She was just lucky the Smythe Foundation had decided, when the evidence for all the unusual unsolvable crimes outgrew its last warehouse, to move the repository into new, spacious digs and to create a staff of trained archivists to curate the repository. They were only a staff of three in an old humongous distribution warehouse in the middle of Virginia, but it was still a job she would have dreamed of having if she had known such a job existed.

And the coolest part was they were also the repository for retired equipment and all kinds of cool gadgets. Because the Smythe Foundation was raising funds to build a museum devoted to the history of the FBI, including all the equipment they had used through the years, they also decided to buy stuff for the museum that were missing from the collection.

Paula wasn't complaining. New technologies and scientific breakthroughs were blowing open cold cases every day. They just had to have a case to use all the new-fangled stuff on.

The Repository of Unusual Unsolvable Crimes was hers now. And she was going to solve some unsolvable crimes, by golly.

Chapter 2

CUTTY SLOWED DOWN as they rounded the curve, the Jeep's tires kicking up white clouds from the newly re-graveled and grated road. She hated the larger chunks of fresh gravel before enough traffic broke them down.

"It's just up here." Officer Jen Ritchey spotted the driveway and pointed to the right. Her stringy blond hair was pulled back into a ponytail dangling through the hole in the back of her Lipping Creek Police Department baseball cap.

"I checked the property records and a Harvey Jones lives there."

Cutty turned onto a deeply rutted gravel driveway, and they bumped past a cluster of ancient birch trees to a one-story, wood-frame house that looked as if it hadn't seen fresh paint in years. She parked behind a black SUV with tinted windows.

"Okay, let's see what we've got here," she said as she climbed out of the Jeep.

Jen joined her as she rounded the Jeep, and they walked through the overgrown grass and weeds up to the front door. Despite the appearance of disrepair from a distance, the door and screen door were new and of good quality. Much higher quality than usually found on an old farmhouse in the national forest.

"Interesting," Cutty muttered.

"This is like one of those big city bar-type screen doors." Jen slipped her fingers around the bars. "Not cheap either."

"Think he has something to hide?" Cutty grabbed the handle and pulled. "Locked." She pushed the dirty white doorbell and heard an anemic electronic bleat inside the house.

They waited a few minutes. Cutty wasn't surprised to hear only silence on the other side of the door. The place felt deserted, almost desolate.

"Hmmm." Jen crunched through the leaves to the front picture window. "Guess he likes his privacy." She tried to find a crack in the curtains.

Cutty went to a smaller window. The blinds were closed, and it looked as if a curtain hung behind them. "The windows look new, too. And heavy duty."

They walked around to the back of the house. An over-sized satellite dish sat next to a dilapidated barn.

Jen looked up at it and grimaced. "God forbid they can't get every football game."

Cutty shook her head at one of the stupider displays of what came out of the testosterone-soaked brains of some of the local yokels. "Let's go take a look at the cave."

They tromped on a well-worn path through a sparse grove of beeches—tall and thin with a surprising number of leaves already on the ground. Cutty breathed in the heady aroma of decay and just nature in general. She still sometimes wondered if she had made the right career choice. Park ranger had always run a close first for her. At least the job in Lipping Creek allowed her to indulge her park ranger hankerings and it made her grandfather proud. That meant everything to her.

The pocked cliff face of Gardner Ridge rose up from a mostly dry creek bed. Centuries of intermittent water flow had cut away the rock shelters and the occasional cave used for countless ages by the original inhabitants of this land. The ceilings of the shallow caves were speckled and blotched with pitch from fire pits, and some even had petroglyphs etched on the mottled limestone walls and potsherds and arrowheads littered the sandy ground.

"The cave's this way." Cutty veered to the left as they sloshed across the sand and the rounded stones of the creek bed. Mammoth, irregular boulders had tumbled off the cliff and created narrow passages and formations that were as much an attraction for hikers and climbers as the cliffs and the rock shelters.

Cutty became aware of their footfalls on the soft sand and dry leaves the closer they got to the gaping hole that looked like a dark splotch in the midst of the surrounding rock shelters that sliced into the base of the cliff. She usually felt calm and centered in the silence of nature, but this stillness was unsettling. Too still. Too quiet. Even the birds weren't foraging.

She exchanged glances with Jen, who looked as if she felt it, too. They stepped up to the mouth of the cave and stared inside. Cutty pulled out her camera and snapped several photos.

"Okay," she said in a low voice. For some reason she didn't want to disturb the silence. "What do you see?"

Jen squinted as she studied the cave, which was streaked with intense yellow-white beams from the late afternoon sun. "The padlock is locked." She gazed at the ground. "No animal disturbance. Kind of surprising. There are a bunch of boot prints here." She looked around her feet. "Only two sets going to the gate. One set is like the prints around us. Lightweight hiking boots. The other set looks like sneakers."

"Step back," Cutty said.

They walked into the creek bed, and Cutty snapped several photos of the mess of footprints and the two sets that went to the barred barrier.

"What else do you see?" Cutty asked as they stepped forward to the cave's mouth.

"The bars and the door are new. Looks like something stronger than the usual iron." Jen shaded her eyes. "I see one set of prints inside the cave—the sneakers."

"Yep." Cutty walked to the padlocked gate, followed by Jen.

Cutty took photos of the footprints inside the cave. They were going into the cave and to the line of metal where the right wall curved out of sight. She snapped more photos of the gray, metal object, the sun glinting off of it almost blinding her.

Jen shaded her eyes. "It does look like a door."

Cutty's curiosity was flaming as bright as the metal. What on earth did the owner have in this cave? She dropped her backpack and pulled out her bolt cutter.

Jen crossed her arms and gave Cutty an amused look. "What are we going to tell the owner?"

"That we believed someone was hurt inside his cave, and he wasn't home." Cutty snapped the padlock open. "Too late for second thoughts now." She grinned as she pulled the lock off the tight links and twisted the chain around the bars. She looked at Jen. "Ready?"

Jen sucked in a breath. "Ready."

Cutty pushed the door open. No creak or resistance. Well-oiled and cared for. She stepped into the cave, careful not to disturb the footprints. Jen walked past the gate to the other side of the prints.

Cutty took close-up photos of the footprints and glanced around the ground. "It looks as if it's been swept."

Jen knelt down and gazed at the even sand. "Maybe he sweeps it when he leaves."

"Which means?"

Their eyes met, and they turned to the half-hidden right wall.

Cutty pushed down a rising dread and shook it away. She was just letting her imagination get away from her. She took slow, deliberate steps toward the side of the cave.

"It *is* a door." She frowned in surprise as she approached the open doorway. Whatever was beyond the threshold was blanketed in darkness. "The footprints go one way into a completely black chamber." She took deep breaths to still her pounding heart. She willed her hands not to shake as she concentrated on removing her flashlight from her belt.

Cutty heard Jen, behind her, fumble with her flashlight and her hand slapping it as she caught it before it hit the ground.

Cutty looked back at her. "The first beer's on me."

Jen, eyes wide with controlled fear, nodded. "You bet it is. I expect dinner thrown in."

Cutty tried to give her a brave grin. "You bet."

She turned to the doorway and flicked on her flashlight. She exchanged glances with Jen and raised the beam. The far wall was black. Flat.

She swept the beam to the left. "What the . . . ?"

The biggest flat screen she had ever seen stood in front of the back wall. Rows of rectangular black towers stood perpendicular to the screen with different-colored cables hanging from them. Flat-screen monitors, like computer monitors, were on a narrow table that ran the width of the cave in front of the towers. The whole back half of the cavern was filled with electronic stuff and tangles of wires and cables.

"One, two, three, four computers." Jen moved her beam along the table. Piles of papers and books littered the flat areas around the keyboards.

Cutty held her breath and aimed her light at the ground. Nothing. She moved it left and stopped on a ribbon of dark sand. She slowly followed the ribbon until it expanded into a stain. She let out her breath as her curiosity overtook her again.

"Flash your beam over here," she said, surprised at the steadiness of her voice.

They moved their beams together in intersecting circles of light and stopped on a rumpled black lump blending into the stained sand.

They moved their beams up and then down to reveal the shape of a human. Sprawled face down.

Cutty shut off her flashlight, and Jen quickly doused her light.

"Let's step out of here," Cutty said, really surprised at how steady her voice was.

They backed out of the cavern room. Cutty blinked away the white-out caused by the sun after the near blackness as she took a few seconds to pull together her trembling thoughts.

"Well, you always wanted something more interesting to happen," Jen said in a shaky voice.

Cutty chuckled. "Yeah. Be careful what you wish for. Right?"

"BE CAREFUL WHAT you ask for," Paula muttered for what seemed like her daily mantra.

She had come up with the logical idea that the most recent crimes would be the easiest to solve because the evidence would be fresh. The problem was, she couldn't find the most recent crimes. Until she took over, the repository had been more storage than archive.

Assistant Archivist Brie, tall, almost gangly, in baggy jeans that hung on barely discernible hips, strode toward Paula down the wide, seemingly endless center corridor of the former distribution warehouse. She held a clipboard thick with a messy stack of paper. Her blue afro and dusky skin glistened in the low hanging fluorescent lights of the three-story high ceiling. Paula grinned at her T-shirt that read, "What we believe, we become."—Buddha.

"I come from far off lands." Brie waved her hand behind her. "But, alas, my search for organized knowledge has been unsuccessful."

Paula ran both hands through her short hair and stared up at the ceiling. The endless ceiling, unbroken by the partition walls that stood a good ten to fifteen feet below it, reminded her of the size of her domain and how little control she had over it.

"The most recent was from 1968," Brie said.

"That's even older than bay 5," Paula said.

"The good news is we have only three bays left." Brie did a little dance. "And Jeff's doing bay 6."

Paula, resigned, held out her hand.

Brie grinned as she gave her the clipboard. "We got job security, at least."

Paula snorted a laugh and flipped through the pages, which were the top sheets from each case file folder. She had figured the best way to organize a warehouse full of stuff was to get all the crimes into a database so they had something to work with while inventorying everything related to the crimes and physically organizing them in chronological order. Job security for several lifetimes.

Mr. Frederick Manning, the first repository director, had been a meticulous records keeper. He had been handpicked by the Smythe family to head the archives and pursued the organization and analysis of these crimes with enthusiasm for forty-something years. He had thought that all these crimes needed were logical and thoughtful examination to uncover the key to solving them. But that had been when the archives was in a section of a building in DC, and then spread out into a small warehouse. The next director, Alan Christiansen, appeared to do little more than mark time for fifteen years until retirement, and no one seemed to bother him about accountability. Old man Smythe was still running the Foundation and his enthusiasm for unsolvable crimes tended toward collecting rather than organizing.

During Mr. Christiansen's last year on the job, the repository was moved to this abandoned retail distribution warehouse off highway 29 near Madison, Virginia. All of Mr. Manning's meticulously organized files and crates were put on trucks and dumped into this space, along with Mr. Christiansen's additions to the chaos—all the materials collected during his tenure had been put wherever there was room. His official reports, which Paula read through when she had started the job, indicated more than what he actually did. The well-worn Scrabble games, drawers of crossword puzzles, and an impressive collection of jigsaw puzzles told the real story of how Mr. Christiansen and his small staff had spent their time.

These crimes were not only unusual, they were deemed unsolvable after all. No one would ever know if she and Brie and Jeff spent their days archiving these crimes or playing countless games of Scrabble. She could write anything on a report, and it'd be believed because of the nonproductive precedence of her predecessor.

But she had wanted this job because she wanted, no, she craved the challenge to solve the unsolvable. Like Frederick Manning, she believed these crimes only needed someone to take the time to pull together all the pieces into a logical picture to reveal the missing clues.

"I guess we should start getting them into the computer," she said.

Brie laughed. "Maybe we'll find some more death by sword."

Paula gave her an amused look as they trudged on the concrete floor, polished by countless loaders and warehouse vehicles, toward the workroom. "Who'd have thought there'd be so many people whose weapon of choice was a sword."

"Just the logistics of carrying one around." Brie waved her hand and shrugged. "Unless there's also a high incidence of murders at Renaissance fairs."

"Or Xena conventions."

Brie snorted a laugh.

Jeff shuffled out of bay 6 at the far end of the corridor. He was fussing with the pile of papers on his clipboard, and they flew off and scattered on the floor, some pieces sliding an impressive distance over the slick concrete.

Paula and Brie laughed at his muffled cursing as he twisted around to look at the mess of papers.

Paula stuck her hands into the front pockets of her jeans. "I guess we should help him."

"Yeah, I guess." Brie rocked on her feet.

They exchanged amused looks and trotted down the corridor, picking up errant papers on the way.

Chapter 3

CUTTY SHOOK HER head at the shiny black sedan with windows tinted almost as black pausing in the gravel road. Nothing like being low-keyed.

She waved the sedan into the rutted driveway and then turned away from the suffocating cloud of white dust. The sedan crunched to a stop in the yard next to the van belonging to Dr. Stephens, the county coroner, the county sheriff's car, and her Jeep.

Cutty trotted to the drivers' side and gave Special Agent Mike Grainger an amused look as he unfolded himself out of the car. "I see you decided to travel incognito."

Mike shut the door and patted the hood of the car. "Well, the Bat Mobile's getting an oil change."

Cutty laughed. "Thanks for getting here so fast in a mere mortal vehicle."

Mike, dressed down in an FBI-issue blue polo shirt and jacket and khakis, stretched his back. "You kidding? This case actually sounds interesting."

"Downright weird is more like it." Cutty led the way through clumps of gold-and-brown leaves to the house.

Mike gazed at the door and frowned. "How of a much problem do you have with break-ins around here?"

"Not enough to merit big city-type security doors." Cutty turned and pointed north. "This road dead-ends another mile that way. Only hikers and people making a wrong turn venture down this way."

"Well, he was either extremely paranoid"—Mike rubbed his chin as he studied the steel bars of the security screen door—"or he was doing something he didn't want anyone to see."

Cutty shrugged. "I guess we'll know as soon as we determine if the person in the cave is the owner."

Mike trudged through the leaves to the back of the house. He stopped and stared at the satellite dish. "This looks homemade. Very sophisticated design. Two-way communications by the look of it."

"Wait till you see what's in the cave." Cutty pulled out her camera and took several photos of the dish, making sure to get all the cable connections and controls.

Mike dug the toe of his boot into the ground where the wires coming off of the dish were buried. "This isn't going to the house."

Cutty blinked at him in surprise and knelt down to get a closer look at the furrow of dirt snuggled around a thick cable—going away from the house . . . toward Gardner Ridge. "That actually makes sense." She had wondered how the owner got electricity to the cave and had done a cursory search for buried cables. He had done a good job of concealing them through the forest.

Mike raised an eyebrow. "That must be some mean equipment down there."

"Let's just say, the Bat Mobile wouldn't feel out of place." Cutty nodded at the path into the forest. "After you."

Mike walked past her. "Color me super intrigued."

Cutty grinned as she followed him. She opened her senses to the forest. She grew up exploring the Shawnee National Forest and sometimes she felt as if she knew it on an almost molecular level. The forest was a living organism to her, and it felt . . . disturbed. She had felt it with Jen a couple hours earlier but had meshed it with her own apprehension about their mission.

The stillness hung heavy, like the silence after a hunter's gun shot. The ubiquitous chatter and foraging of birds and tiny critters were absent at a time when it should have been the noisiest—nearing twilight. She'd experienced this kind of stillness once before . . . right before a larger than usual tremor shook the area.

Gardner Ridge rose up in front of them, a mottled gray wall of stone she had found endlessly fascinating when she was young.

"Follow the creek bed to the left." She pointed to where the creek meandered around the bulge of the cliff.

They crunched on the sand and rocks—the noise sounding too loud to Cutty. She looked out into the trees and opened up her hearing. Eerie silence. An impending quake would be too much of a coincidence but she hoped mother nature and nothing more unexplainable and sinister was silencing the forest-dwellers.

They walked to the perimeter of yellow crime tape Jen and Undersheriff Rick were putting up in a semi-circle from the bluff walls about ten feet from the cave on either side. Sheriff Daryll was visiting his sister in Arkansas, so Rick got to be in on all the fun.

"Looks good," Cutty said.

"Thanks, boss." Jen grinned as she lifted the tape to allow them through.

Mike stopped at the mouth of the cave and looked at all the footprints in the sand.

"I took photos before we disturbed everything," Cutty said.

Mike nodded. "Good. How many sets going in and out?" He ran his hand over the bars and lifted the chain and padlock. "Seriously heavy duty."

"Rampant anti-social tendencies." Cutty strolled into the cave and faced him. "One set of prints. Going into the cave."

Mike looked up from inspecting the padlock. "What?"

"One set. Into the cave. Tennis shoes." Cutty crossed her arms and arched an eyebrow.

Mike cocked his head. "Say what?"

"You heard me," Cutty said.

Mike opened and closed his mouth several times. Cutty knew he was running through all the possible scenarios. She and Jen had gone through as many as they could think of while waiting for the coroner.

"Let's see"—she put her index finger on her thumb—"the perpetrator would have had to be able to go through the gate without disturbing the prints already there and sweep only her tracks."

"Her?" Mike asked.

"The hikers heard a female voice answer the man." Cutty slapped index fingers together. "Or she had to enter the cave before the victim, cover her tracks while entering and exiting." She walked up to the bars. "The hitch in any scenario is that she had to get through a door that was padlocked. So she could have a key. The padlock shows no evidence of being tampered with."

"So the padlock was locked when the hikers got here," Mike said.

"Yep." Cutty gave him a wry look. "Guess you should see the crime scene."

"Guess?" Mike grinned.

Cutty made an elaborate bow and wave of her hand. "After you."

Mike walked past her and stepped into the side cave. Cutty and Jen had set up spotlights just inside the door that illuminated the whole chamber.

Mike looked around in wide-eyed amazement and focused on the black screen that dominated the back wall. "Wow. People will do anything to get cable TV in the sticks."

"And not want anyone else to watch it either," Cutty said.

Dr. Irene Stephens looked up from inspecting the body and gave them a wry look. "Ya think?"

Cutty studied the body, now turned over and revealing a surprisingly young man with a mild almost milquetoast face and thinning dishwater hair. Not the grizzled unabomber type she had envisioned. Served her right for giving in to stereotypes. The man didn't look familiar, which was odd in itself, given she was sure she had seen everyone who lived within her jurisdiction at least once. At the gas station, the grocery store, or buying stamps at the post office. She wasn't even sure if she'd seen his SUV on the road.

"This setup is pretty impressive." Mike went to Dr. Stephens and looked down at the body. "What do we have here?"

Dr. Stephens sat back on her heels. "Definitely not natural causes."

Cutty rolled her eyes. "Please tell me it's self-inflicted."

Dr. Stephens gazed at her over half-glasses. "See a weapon around here? Cause of death is a single wound to the heart."

"Shot?" Mike asked.

"Stabbed."

"Stabbed?" Mike studied the pattern of blood on the ground. "What position was he in?"

"On his stomach. I took plenty of photos." Cutty pulled her camera from her pack and sifted through the images on the LED display. She found the best body shot and handed the camera to Mike.

He spent several minutes looking back and forth between the photo and the real body. He zoomed in and around the image and finally handed the camera back to Cutty.

He went back to the doorway and faced the body. "If the knife had been thrown, it would have embedded in him, and he would have fallen backward or slumped down." He pretended to throw a knife. "The perpetrator would have been able to pull the knife out without leaving much evidence and could have quickly covered her prints."

Cutty nodded. "True. But that's not what happened."

"Uh, no." Mike rested his cheek on his hand as he stared at the body and the area around it. "Okay. If the perpetrator stabbed him at close range, she would have had to pull the knife out and help him fall face down. Which means there may be evidence on the man's clothing."

"But what about blood splatters from pulling out a knife? Wouldn't his face be splattered? And wouldn't there be drops from the knife as the perpetrator is lowering him with one hand and holding the knife in the other?" Cutty turned around and took in the cavern ground. "Shouldn't there be a lot more evidence of blood around?" She pointed at a pair of undisturbed tennis shoe prints. "How could she sweep the sand so clean and not disturb those prints? There would have been blood splatters in the prints closest to the body."

"There was only a single set of footprints?"

"Yep. Just like out there." Cutty nodded at the door. She browsed through the photos on her camera. "Here's a good shot, before we walked in the first time."

Mike took the camera and stared at the photo, zoomed in on it, and then looked at the ground around him. Cutty had never seen him so confounded.

"One more thing," she said. "If she stabbed him and cleaned up so there wasn't any trace, she would have made noises. The hikers said there was dead silence after the man screamed. And they waited for fifteen minutes in the woods as still as before a tornado. And country quiet isn't like city quiet, and caves are like echo chambers. You can hear bats scraping the ceiling deep inside a cave."

"Maybe the perp heard the hikers outside," Mike said.

"Maybe. But they heard nothing. No squishing, falling, shuffling, nothing. Dead silence." Cutty grabbed Mike's shoulder and pretended to thrust a knife into his heart and held her fist against his chest. "Could the perp stand completely frozen for fifteen minutes after stabbing a victim? Holding him before pulling out the knife? Blood oozing out of the wound, creating a different pattern on his clothes than what's there? Blood flowing over the hilt of her knife and her hand, dripping onto the ground and her shoes, making a big, bloody mess?" She released Mike and stepped back. "I guess you'll have fun re-creating all the scenarios in your lab."

"Well, this cave is toward the back of the outer cave and to the side," Mike said.

"And the hikers said the voices sounded so close they could have been coming from just inside." Cutty gave Mike a sheepish look. "Jen and I did a little experiment of our own while we waited for Doc."

Mike shook his head, amused. "Why am I not surprised?"

"We were curious. What can I say?" Cutty shrugged. "Anyway, cave acoustics can be unpredictable. I stayed in here, and Jen went out to where the hikers hid behind the trees just across the creek. I shuffled my boots like I was wiping away prints. I shrugged in and out of my jacket, which is like the jacket material on the victim. I pulled my backpack off and on and paced around a bit. Jen could hear most of these sounds. The rounded back wall of the outer cavern seems to act like an echo chamber."

"And that door was open when the hikers were here?" Mike pointed at the thick metal door.

"Yep."

Dr. Stephens packed up her equipment, stood, and stretched out her back. "I have a couple more things to add to the puzzle." She nodded at the body. "It hasn't shown any sign of decay or disturbance. Out here, the critters and insects would have gotten to it pretty quickly—at least the things small enough to get through the bars. I couldn't begin to tell you the time of death based on the state of the body alone. The condition of the blood is far worse than the body." She knelt down and carefully pulled the shirt away from over the heart. "This wound is meticulously clean and seems to have held the shape of the weapon that created it."

Cutty stared at a slit that had to be at least four inches. Kind of wide for a knife. And the slit was parallel to the ground. Awkward to hold for most knife handles. The clean gape in the skin was maybe a half inch in the middle and tapered to an edge on either side.

She looked up. "Double-edged." She took several photos of the wound.

Dr. Stephens nodded. "Looks like it. What kind of knife do you think made this?"

Mike knelt on the other side of the body and peered at the wound. "Looks like a good-size blade. Knives aren't really my specialty."

"Well"—Dr. Stephens stood up—"if I didn't know better, I'd say it wasn't a knife at all."

Mike frowned up at her. His expression was curious . . . and something else. Cutty's imagination sparked a bit. What could he be thinking?

"What do you think made this wound?" Did Mike sound a bit wary?

"Just going by the size and angle of entry, how the bottom part of the wound is weighted . . ." Dr. Stephens cocked her head. "I'd say a sword."

Cutty let out a snort. "A sword?"

Mike rose to his feet and ran both hands through his close-trimmed hair. He heaved a deep sigh and turned to the bank of electronic equipment. He walked along it, as if seeking some kind of answer there.

He finally turned to them, resignation on his face. "You know the old puzzle about the man who hangs himself in an empty room with the door locked on the inside?"

"Dry ice," Cutty and Dr. Stephens said together.

"Well, there have been a series of murders through the years involving what looks like a sword wound and no apparent evidence. Just like this one." Mike gazed at the body and shook his head. "It looks like I won't have the opportunity to work on a more interesting case after all."

"Why not?" Cutty took a closer look at the power cord high on the right wall. Somehow it ran all the way back to the house. The ends dangled from clips nailed into the stone. Someone would have had to drag a chair from the table to the wall to slice the line with a knife. But a sword . . . She stood on her tip toes and peered up at the wall. A sword could have done the job.

"All of these cases go to a special division." Mike shrugged and seemed to recover his good humor. "And I was looking forward to solving a nice out of the ordinary mystery."

PAULA, PERCHED ON a stool at her favorite worktable, looked up from the pile of printouts she was highlighting with an assortment of colors. Sometimes the best method of finding relationships between crimes and categorizing them was the old-fashioned way—color coding.

Dull clicks hit the concrete at a sprinter's pace and came closer from outside in the corridor. Sounded like Brie's cowboy boots.

"What the . . . ?"

Brie ran into the workroom between the flimsy cube-farm partitions that passed for interior walls in the warehouse.

"Where's the fire?" Paula pushed up her wire rims and focused on a very excited Brie.

"One huge truck, like a Bud-Light-at-a-football-game-size truck is backing up to bay 7," Brie gasped out in short breaths.

"Has there been an outbreak of unusual, unsolvable crimes?" Paula slipped off the stool and followed Brie into the corridor. The beep, beep, beep of a truck backing up echoed around the building.

"I bet they found more oddball crimes while cleaning out a basement or something," Brie said. "I mean that only makes sense."

"Just when we have everything in the computers they dump more on us." Despite her words, Paula felt a tinge of excitement. Maybe the truck contained the remains of the most interesting, most unusual, most unsolvable crimes.

They walked through the gap between the partitions that separated the corridor from bay 7—one of several completely empty bays in the facility. One metal rolling door on the cinder block wall was wide open. Jeff hovered just out of the way as he watched four workers in dark gray coveralls unhook the back of the truck and lower the gate.

Paula walked up to Jeff, who was jumping from foot to foot—his hyperactive tendencies on serious overdrive.

"What do we have here?" she asked.

Jeff handed her a manilla envelope. "A new crime."

Paula watched as the men carried off the truck piece after piece of electronics, cables, monitors, keyboards . . . and piled them along the partition. "This is for one crime?"

"Yep." Jeff bounced on the balls of his flip flops.

Brie sauntered up to them with arms crossed. "Looks like Best Buy coughed up a digital hairball."

"Maybe we can rig up a new game of Pong from all this," Paula said.

Brie gave her a wry look. "If it works like everything else we've tried to put together, that'd be a major accomplishment."

Paula grinned as she opened the envelope and pulled out several paper-clipped sheets. The top sheet was a report stating that this case had been assigned to the Repository of Unusual Unsolvable Crimes according to the factors delineated in document number yadda yadda yadda. She flipped to the next page. The single-page crime report. She glanced through the particulars. Possible weapon, sword.

Another one? She frowned at the stamped date. "What's the date today?"

Jeff and Brie looked at each other and pulled out their phones.

"October twenty-sixth," they said together.

"When do you think this crime was committed?" Paula asked.

Jeff scrunched his forehead as he watched the workers pull the last pieces from the truck. "At least a couple of months ago, if they got to it in a timely manner. Depends on the number of leads they had to follow up on and the amount of evidence . . ."

Paula flipped through the pages. Coroner's report. Evidence sheet. Reports from the local police chief and FBI agent. The longest report was three pages—from the local chief. The evidence sheet was a signed form with the words "No evidence found" typed on it.

"No leads. No evidence. A body with a sword wound through the heart." Paula looked up at them. "Sound familiar?"

"Another death by sword?" Brie asked in disbelief.

Jeff scratched his head. "Someone sure has a Conan—"

"Or Xena—"

"Complex."

"So how recent is this crime?" Brie asked.

"The crime was committed on the twenty-first," Paula said.

"Of October?" Jeff squeaked.

"Of this year?" Brie's eyes widened as the workers carried a satellite dish from the truck. "Glory be, we'll finally be able to get Showtime."

Jeff gazed at the dish. "Showtime? We'll be able to make alien contact."

Paula slipped the papers back into the envelope. "Something about this crime deemed it immediately unsolvable without even a cursory investigation. They just tagged it, logged it, and shipped it to us."

"So, are we going to work on it?" Brie asked. "Being the most recent and all?"

Paula cocked her head. "What do you think?"

"I'm thinking, hell yeah."

Jeff whooped and hollered, startling the men from the truck.

"It's fresh, untouched, and it's all ours," Paula said. "We find Conan, and maybe we'll solve the whole death by sword mystery."

Chapter 4

CUTTY SAT ON the bench in front of the police department. They had experienced the apex of Indian Summer last weekend, and this weekend the clouds hung low in an angry lead gray, the temperature a breezy fifty degrees. She could smell rain on the gusts of wind. The hardcore hikers were still getting lunch from Marge's, but the stream of cars and bicycles into the state park was intermittent. Hiking in cool, overcast weather had its own charm that she often preferred to sunshiny days.

One week ago, she had found a dead body in a cave just a few miles from where she sat. Harvey Jones, the owner of the property, had been born in Anna, in the neighboring county, but had spent most of his adult life in Washington DC as a government computer geek. Then two years ago, he quit his job and moved back to Southern Illinois.

Did he get lucky to find property with a cave when he was looking for one? Or did he wait until he found property with a cave? Did it matter?

She gave her head a shake. "I've got to stop thinking about it. It's not my case anymore."

It killed her that she'd never know the resolution of the mystery in the cave. She refused to become one of those doddering, retired police chiefs who bored everyone with the story of finding a body in a cave and never knowing what happened but had a lifetime of increasingly bizarre theories about it.

"No, I'll just be a loony young chief driving everyone crazy." She laughed. "I'm already talking to myself."

She watched the city banner proclaiming Lipping Creek, Gateway to White Bluffs State Park billow between the dowels that held it taut on the lamppost across the street. The wind gusts were getting serious.

"Hang it all." She jumped to her feet and pushed open the door. "I'll be back," she yelled, then let the door slam behind her as she hurried around the block to her Jeep.

She drove out to the gravel lane that went nowhere—that had a single residence on it. Maybe Harvey Jones had consciously looked for the perfect property to perform whatever nefarious business he had been into.

The grooves in the gravel were almost flat from a truck that had rivaled those Coke trucks that were always threatening to take out four lanes of traffic, the stop light, and half a building when making a right turn from a lane of oncoming traffic.

She parked in the driveway and trudged around the house past the torn-up ground where the satellite dish had been.

A stream of movers in Hazmat-type getups had hauled all the stuff out of the cave, the house, and everything around the house, including the SUV, like a highly disciplined hive of worker ants. Then they had shut the truck doors with an echoing bang, climbed into the cabs and the SUVs, and left in a slow procession of the white truck and blacks SUVs that seemed to float on the cloud of gravel dust—eerie, funereal. Cutty's shoulders had twitched from the chill down her spine. By the time the dust had settled, even the engines were a distant memory and the forest sounds returned.

Now . . . now . . . the forest felt normal. The jays squawked, the catbirds threw leaves while foraging, the sparrows chattered as they flitted among the trees.

She stopped, let the echo from her crunching footfalls die out, and listened. Yep. Normal. She looked up into the almost bare trees stretching like elongated humans to the sky. Vireos flitted around the bare canopy. She could just see the blue-gray back of a white-breasted nuthatch crab-walking down a trunk.

Normal.

She'll never take that word for granted again. How many times had she gone out on a call to investigate something suspicious and everything was normal? As if nothing could have recently disturbed a scene. Normal was the natural state of things, and things just wanted to get back to it as fast as possible.

But . . . she walked, keeping her footfalls quiet so not to disturb the pleasing sounds around her . . . this disturbance had lasted from the time of the crime to the removal of all remnants from the scene of the crime. Like a force had blanketed the area until all traces of the disturbance were gone.

God. She could give herself vertigo with all her up and down, head-spinning thoughts. Or was that whiplash?

She followed along the creek until she got to a rough line of rocks that conveniently spanned the creek, and hikers used after rains. A thunderstorm had rolled in the night before, filling the creek enough to soak her boots if she stepped into it. She hopped from rock to rock across the creek and walked on the narrow trail close to the bluff. She ducked into shallow caves with ceilings black with soot and skirted the slick rocks on thin strips of squishy sand against the cliff face. She finally squeezed past a pool of water into the mouth of the cave.

She hadn't visited the cave after the truck and SUVs left two days earlier. The sky had darkened by that time, and she had convinced herself the case was no longer hers, and she should just walk away.

She sighed as she studied the now wide-open cave. She dug her fingers into the indentations where the bars had been embedded into the rock—the only evidence that a barred gate had been there.

The soaked sand squished beneath her boots as she walked into the cave. Flash floods easily filled the cave with water. Through the years, she had seen as much as a foot of water lapping the cavern walls. She pulled her flashlight from her belt and flashed its beam around.

The atmosphere felt different. Before, the air had been heavy and almost foreboding. Now it was . . . normal . . . almost welcoming. The way all caves felt to her. Friendly orifices beckoning her to explore.

She went to the wall with the opening—now just a gap. The metal door was gone, and only a line of chiseled marks remained where it had been connected to the rough, uneven stone.

She stood at the threshold and stared into the darkness. Again, she didn't feel anything foreboding. She flicked on her flashlight and aimed it into the cavern. Empty. She walked in and illuminated the whole cavern, bit by bit. No trace, except where the hooks had hung the power line.

Except . . . she sucked in her breath . . . a deep thin incision in the rock, ragged on the outer edges and clean on the inside. Like it had been . . . slit.

She stood on her tiptoes, using the wall as support, but she couldn't get a better look. She set her camera to close-up and held it over her head and squinted at the black LED. She prayed as she clicked off a few shots in a blinding flurry of flashes. If the perpetrator had cut the power cord with her sword, she could have gotten the sword stuck in the sandstone and had struggled to get it out.

She checked her photos and thanked the goddess of exposed light that her aim had been right on the money.

She ran the flashlight over the stone below the incision. Did the perpetrator brace herself with her hands on the wall? How clear would fingerprints be on a rough sandstone surface? She dropped the beam, and something flashed in the sand.

"What the . . . ?" She knelt and brushed away the wet sand. The object was metallic but too thick and irregularly shaped to be a piece of wiring. She pulled a plastic evidence bag from her backpack and scooped up the metal shard without touching it.

"How did the FBI miss this?"

She squinted up and lit the incision with the flashlight. Unless it had been lodged in the wall and fell after they left.

Which meant . . . She held up the bag and shone the flashlight on it. Could be a part of a blade. She pushed down her rising excitement and took a deep breath.

"Just take it back and study it logically at the office."

She flashed her light around the chamber.

"I guess I'll just have to live with never knowing the answer to the mystery. But it doesn't hurt to cover all the bases."

She grinned as she pulled from her backpack a Styrofoam blob painted to look like the white-pocked rock of the cave. Her grandfather, frustrated with the vandalism of the more popular rock shelters and caves, had wished there was a way to hide cameras in the caves without all the wires. Technology finally caught up with his idea and Cutty surprised him one Sunday afternoon with a do-it-yourself party of creating remote cameras disguised as rocks. Since the cave was out of range from any Wi-Fi signal, someone could just stop by every few days and switch out the memory cards and batteries if needed.

She illuminated the walls all around the cavern and walked to the side opposite from where she found the metal shard. She ran the beam of the flashlight at about chest level and inspected a few deeper pock marks.

"That looks pretty good." She took a Styrofoam blob, turned it so a small hole faced outward, and carefully shoved it into the craggy hole. She smoothed the edges into the surrounding rock as best she could and stood back. "Good enough. No one's going to be looking for a hidden camera in the wall."

She was close enough to pick up a Bluetooth signal from the camera on her phone. She stared at a black screen and then she remembered to switch the mode to infrared. There she was as big as life.

She did a little joyful shake of her shoulders. Technology always surprised her when it worked, especially on the first try.

She took another Styrofoam blob from her backpack, stood in the middle of the cave, and turned with her flashlight shining on the wall. The back was the most logical choice for catching the faces of anyone who entered.

She went to the wall, found a deep hole, and shoved the other blob into it, then smoothed the edges so it blended as much as possible. She stepped back and lit it with her flashlight. "That'll work."

She put her third camera to the side of the cave entrance.

She tested the last two cameras on her phone and gave the cave one last sweep with the flashlight. She stared at the back wall for several seconds, knowing that leaving meant walking away from this mystery forever and every cell in her body hated that idea.

PAULA BOUNCED ON the uneven back road as she drove the only hybrid she could rent at the St. Louis airport. She actually welcomed the winding two-lane road after a couple of hours on the Interstate. Highway driving was so boring.

She had always thought of Illinois as flat with miles and miles of cornfields and Chicago skyscrapers looming in the distance. Never had she imagined this beautiful hilly countryside with farms and endless forest, with red and orange leaves blanketing the lawns and fields this time of year—much like central Indiana where she went to school. Not a place she'd imagine as a scene for an unsolvable crime . . . with a sword. Southern Illinois reminded her of the mountains of Virginia, except more isolated and less farms and houses doting the countryside.

She turned onto a blacktopped road with the paint so fresh it sparkled white and yellow in the sunshine. A sign said that Lipping Creek and White Bluffs State Park were just ahead. Signs of civilization took the form of a rambling shack with polished wood carvings of bears, dragons, Buddhas, cats, chess pieces for giants . . . hundreds of pieces of wood art from an endless imagination and an enviable skill with a chain saw.

A small gas station/repair shop inhabited a building that looked like one of those ancient one-pump gas stations from the early twentieth century. It blended into the narrow blocks of turn-of-the-twentieth-century storefronts that climbed up a hill topped with a white-steepled church. A round green area surrounding a statue in a fountain spread out in front of the church, and the road split to go around it. She looked up the cross streets. One side was a steep hill with houses looking on top of each other. The other side was a flat couple of blocks of houses and neat front lawns with a patchwork of leaves, dormant gardens, and quaint iron fences. A steep hill with exposed bluff walls rose up beyond those streets.

She moved along in the stream of cars creeping through the town. Most of the cars turned right up ahead where the road split to go around the circle of green toward the densely wooded bluffs that almost towered over the town.

She spotted the police department—a simple storefront between what looked like an outdoors store and a café. Clumps of hikers, families, and bicyclists were scattered around the block, eating, drinking, and standing in a line that snaked out of the café.

"Must be a good place to grab a sandwich."

What made her think the village would be dead on the weekend? Her own research had told her that Lipping Creek was like Sperryville, Virginia—the gateway to all kinds of outdoor activity. Of course, she had never imagined Southern Illinois to be such a mecca for outdoor enthusiasts, even after studying the Google maps of the state park bordering Lipping Creek.

She steered around the block and pulled in front of a Victorian house—stately with a quiet dignity. She jumped out of the car and stretched her back and legs. The day was cool but amazingly clear—the crispness refreshing. She took in the block of Victorians, painted in bright colors with contrasting trims. Flower gardens dominated the front lawns, now dormant but still holding the promise of what the block probably looked like in spring—like the busiest, gaudiest Impressionist painting.

Paula admired towns that took pride in their history and preserved such stately remnants of their past. She loved history, period. She always felt as if she trod back in time on streets like this one. Even with the overflow of cars parked in every possible space.

She gave a friendly nod to the cluster of bicyclists on the corner. They were gesturing over a map and pointing in different directions. Several kids ran past her, ahead of their rambling parents. She paused at the table in front of the outdoors shop. Mostly canteens and other hiking gear were on display.

A bell tinkled as she pushed open the door of the police department. The black and white floor tiles looked original to the building and the walls were exposed, painted brick. A bench that was probably an old church pew lined one wall and a crescent-shaped service counter extended out from the opposite wall. A young woman with long blonde hair pulled back in a ponytail glanced up from behind the counter and then stood. She looked as if she could be a volleyball player—long and lean, with a friendly open face.

"May I help you?" she asked.

"Hi, I'm Paula Reisling, Director of the Repository of Unusual Unsolvable Crimes. I'm looking for Chief Catherine Downes."

The young woman grinned—probably glad Paula wasn't another visitor asking for directions. "I'll let her know you're here." She squeezed out between the wall and the counter with enviable grace and trotted down a narrow corridor.

Paula couldn't help her smile. She found the informality of village life as refreshing as it was quaint.

The young woman emerged from the corridor and squeezed back behind the counter. Another woman—probably early thirties, medium height, short scattered brown hair, and a friendly open face—stepped into the lobby. She wore khakis and a crew neck sweater with her badge attached. Paula was glad she had opted for lightweight hiking boots, jeans, and a sweater underneath a bomber jacket.

The woman held out her hand. "I'm Chief Catherine Downes. Everyone calls me Cutty."

Paula shook her hand. Even Cutty's grasp was warm and friendly. "Paula Reisling. And I'm just Paula to everyone, except when I want to yank somebody's chain."

Cutty cocked her head. "I bet it's a lot more fun to mess with someone's mind working for something with Unusual Unsolvable Crimes in the name than as a small-town police chief."

"Maybe we should compare notes. I'm sure someone somewhere has gotten the government to fund a study on it."

Cutty grinned with curiosity in her eyes as she politely stepped aside and gestured at the corridor. "Let's go to my office so we can chat. Last door on the left."

Paula walked past Cutty into the narrow corridor that ran the length of the building to the back door. She took in the framed posters of breathtaking cliffs and rock formations that lined the walls. The wainscoting was an interesting design touch, and Dutch doors opened to rooms that looked more like turn-of-the-twentieth-century clerk offices than a twenty-first century police department. Lots of solid dark wood and leather, with bookshelves lining the walls filled with thick bound volumes.

She entered a sizable chamber that boasted a back window that overlooked an alley and a side view and backyards of a block of Victorians. The heavy wood and leather office chair would not have been out of place in her grandfather's law office. The wall shelves were filled with books. The only concession to the twenty-first century was the phone system and the flat computer screen and keyboard on what used to be a wing reserved for a typewriter.

"Have a seat," Cutty said, coming in behind her. She indicated a pair of black leather chairs in front of a small stone fireplace with a fire crackling in it on the outer wall. The chairs were facing each other as much as the fire.

Paula settled in a chair. Comfortable, warm. She tried not to sink into it and groan with pleasure.

Cutty went to a shelf next to the fireplace and opened a small wooden door, revealing what looked like a coffee maker on top of a teapot. She held up a couple of tea bags. "All I have is tea. It has caffeine in it."

"Tea is fine," Paula said. In fact, it sounded perfect for the setting.

"Milk, sugar?"

"Both, please."

Cutty prepared two mugs of tea. The aroma alone sent Paula into a heavenly haze. She always loved the smell of English Breakfast.

Cutty handed her a mug and sat in the other chair. She crossed her legs, sat back with her elbows on the arms of the chair, and held the mug in both hands. "So, how can I help you?"

Paula pulled herself from the warm comfort of the chair and tea. "I'm the Director of the Repository for Unusual Unsolvable Crimes."

Cutty gave her an amused look. "Sounds like something out of Monty Python."

Paula was used to that reaction. "Sometimes it feels like something out of Monty Python."

Realization flickered across Cutty's face. "Does this have to do with the murder in the cave?"

Paula nodded. "The very same. The case has been sent to us."

"That explains why I couldn't turn over possible evidence to Mike Grainger," Cutty said.

"Right." Paula sipped her tea to cover her surprise that Cutty had some kind of evidence. "The case met the criteria of a certain class of crime that automatically relegates it to the repository."

Cutty eyed Paula as she sipped her tea. "You mean the man hanging in a locked empty room kind of criteria?" Her eyes danced with an intelligent twinkle.

Paula looked at her, surprised. "That's a part of the criteria."

"Let me guess." Cutty held up a finger and cocked her head as if thinking. "A sword is involved."

Paula took a long sip of tea as she pushed down her racing thoughts. This chief seemed to know a lot about a case that had no investigation.

"You had to be there," Cutty said.

"The file said that photographs may exist of the crime scene," Paula said.

"By the time I went through them, no one seemed to want them," Cutty said.

"Are they your evidence?"

Cutty shrugged with a half-smile dancing on her lips.

Paula narrowed her eyes. "Are you playing hard to get?"

Cutty grinned. "I never give away all my secrets on the first interview with directors of places with weird names."

Paula laughed and put her empty mug on the table between the chairs. "Well, we're researching this case, while it's still fresh."

Cutty frowned. "The crime just happened. Why wouldn't you be researching it?"

Paula took a deep breath. "Cases that receive this kind of designation are not pursued. At least, they've never been pursued until we decided to delve deeper into it."

"And what's so special about now?"

Paula shrugged. "I'm in charge."

Cutty's eyes sparked, like Paula imagined her own eyes looked when a challenge was building up inside of her. Feisty. She liked that. And kind of cute in an impish sort of way.

"And now someone may not get away with murder," Cutty said.

Paula sat forward. "That's how it used to be. I'm starting a new tradition. We're going to start researching some of these unsolvable crimes so they can be solved."

Cutty gave a single nod of solidarity. "Good for you."

"So, I'm here to visit the scene of the crime and to collect any evidence you have," Paula said.

Cutty put her mug on the table and steepled her fingers with her elbows on the chair's arms. "You know, I like the challenge of a good mystery. And this is one heck of a mystery."

"I took this job to have the opportunity to solve what everyone else deemed unsolvable," Paula said.

"Sounds like a dream job." Cutty grabbed the arms of the chair, ready to stand. "I guess we should get to the cave before we lose our light."

Paula grinned. She could barely keep down her anticipation.

Chapter 5

CUTTY'S MIND WAS chasing so many thoughts, she couldn't slow them down or straighten them out as they headed back to town. She was dying to know what a Repository of Unusual Unsolvable Crimes looked like. Was it something like the last scene of *Raiders of the Lost Ark*? That would be so cool. She was also curious about this geeky but likable woman who, she found out, was actually an archivist.

She turned onto the blacktop. Paula, feet up on the dashboard, was entering notes into her tablet. Paula had been shocked that all the stuff delivered to the repository had been in that cavern and took up only half of it. She then snapped a lot of photos and asked a lot of questions.

Paula's enthusiasm was unabashed like Cutty's tended to be when she was really caught up in something.

"So there weren't any reports of anything suspicious?" Paula looked up at Cutty.

"You saw where he lived." Cutty shrugged. "Only hikers and people taking a wrong turn end up on that road. There aren't any trailheads off it, so only those hikers who know the lay of the land, park where the road ends to get to one of the trails maybe a quarter mile into the forest."

Paula cocked her head. "Sounds like an activity you're familiar with."

Cutty grinned. "I've done it a few times."

"A lot of hikers go past that cave?" Paula asked.

"Relatively speaking? It's not one of the more heavily traveled parts of the forest." Cutty waved to a group of bicyclists who were pulled over in one of the trailhead turnouts. "The hikers who reported the crime were Sierra Clubbers. They know where all the off-the-beaten-trail petroglyphs and other hidden treasures of the forest are. Most of these things aren't on maps to protect them."

Paula nodded as she fingered in a few more notes. "So. What do you think?"

Cutty glanced at her. "Huh?"

"Do you think it's unsolvable?"

Cutty guided the Jeep around several hairpin curves dug into a skeletal forest that was thick and lush in the summertime as she wound through the back way into White Bluffs State Park. She pulled into a gravel parking lot full of cars and people. The bluffs loomed just beyond a picnic area, inviting visitors to explore the deep hollows and hidden waterfalls.

She turned to Paula with one arm on the steering wheel and the other arm against the back of her seat. "You know, I don't know if it's solvable or not, but I'd give anything to be a part of the team trying to solve it."

Paula gave her a long look. "Sounds like it's captured your curiosity."

Cutty laughed. "I've been pretty much obsessing over it. My brain won't let it go."

"Well, we are an archives, and people can use our materials in their research." Paula rubbed her chin. "Of course, being overseen by the Smythe Foundation with special instructions from the Justice Department, there *are* certain levels of security."

Cutty started up the engine and looked at Paula. "What's the security level for the Repository of Unusual Unsolvable Crimes."

Paula waggled her head. "We have a lock on the front door and some rather creative security alarms, but the stray cats still find their way in to volunteer for rodent control."

Cutty bit her lip to keep from smiling and pulled out of the parking lot. "So that means I can help out."

Paula shrugged. "I would welcome the extra hand . . . and curious mind, not to mention practical expertise in actual law enforcement." She tucked her tablet into her messenger bag. "The archives were originally funded by Seymour Richard Smythe, a rich crime enthusiast. He formed a foundation to run it, and the Justice Department was more than happy to unload their growing collection of artifacts from unsolvable crimes. So, we're archivists with no law enforcement experience."

"I might have a piece of evidence." Cutty drove past a gravel parking lot with a sheer cliff rising up beyond it. Several rappellers were bouncing down the rock wall on ropes. "Not the photographs."

Paula stared at her. "Real evidence?"

"Maybe."

"What kind of evidence?" Paula shifted around to face Cutty.

Cutty pulled onto the main blacktop that went out of the park. "Well, it's probably nothing. But . . ." She shrugged and gave Paula a side glance.

Amusement sparkled in Paula's eyes. "You know, we archivists have ways of prying information from reluctant people."

Cutty suppressed a smile. "Oh, yeah? Any of them fun?"

Paula chuckled. "Well, I could force the reluctant holder of possible evidence to let me buy dinner."

Cutty pulled to the side of the road and turned to Paula. "Do you like Italian?"

"You bet."

PAULA GRINNED AS she climbed out of the Jeep in a typical downtown with a university just down the street. Clumps of students surged up and down the street between the crowded bars and eateries. An old-style movie theatre had a line of waiting people going around the corner. The night air had just enough nip in it to remind her that winter was closing in.

"I love it," she said.

Cutty gave her a quizzical look.

"Reminds me of where I went to college," Paula said.

"I went to school here." Cutty shrugged into her jacket. "I know all the good places to eat." She joined Paula on the sidewalk. "Where'd you go to school?"

"Indiana University," Paula said.

"Fellow Midwesterner." Cutty nodded her approval. "This way. Pietra's is on the corner."

They walked past the noisy bars with the neon beer brands in the window. The reek of beer wafted out and hung on the cold air from the doors constantly opening and closing.

Paula looked in a restaurant window at the crush of patrons squeezed around tables and in booths. Cutty opened the door to the place. The wall of tomato sauce and cheesy aromas smacked Paula in her senses' memories. Talk about having college flashbacks.

They walked past a pizza-making counter to the main dining room— red leather booths with red-checkered tablecloths hugging the walls, and tables pushed together and filled with large, rambunctious groups in the middle of the floor. The clientele was a mix grad students and families as well as undergrads.

"Everyone who comes home for the holidays eats here at some point," Cutty said. "And everyone seems to meet people they haven't seen in ages."

"Do you call this place home?" Paula asked as a young woman— definitely a student—led them to a booth.

"My parents are professors, so I pretty much grew up here," Cutty said. "I went to the University of Illinois for grad school, but somehow ended up back here."

Paula settled into the red leather and brass-studded booth across from Cutty. The server placed menus in front of them.

"Can I get you something to drink?" she asked.

"Blue Moon, please," Cutty said.

"Sounds good." Paula nodded.

"Two Blue Moons coming right up." The server walked away.

"What do you recommend?" Paula opened the menu. Typical Italian fare with a page devoted to pizza.

"Everything's good," Cutty said. "I can only vouch for the meatless stuff."

Paula glanced up. "Vegetarian?"

"Yep." Cutty shrugged. "Second generation."

"Well, I can't say you've missed anything," Paula said. "I've never been what you'd call an enthusiastic meat eater."

Cutty put her menu down. "So would you be interested in splitting a large thick-crust vegetarian pizza?"

"Sounds great." Paula closed her menu.

The server arrived with their bottles of Blue Moons with orange slices perched on the lips of a pair of frosted glasses. Cutty ordered the pizza, and the server disappeared into the crowd.

Paula filled her glass and squeezed the orange into it. She took a long sip and let the soothing blend of wheat, orange, and alcohol relax her for what she hoped would be an entertaining and enlightening conversation.

"So," she began, "I've held up my end of the bargain."

Cutty sipped her beer and cocked her head. "I haven't seen actual money on the table yet."

Paula met Cutty's gaze, which was filled with a twinkling challenge. She pulled her wallet from her back pocket and laid two twenties on the table.

Cutty raised an eyebrow. "This isn't a big city pizza joint."

Paula replaced a twenty with two fives and lifted an eyebrow.

Cutty poked at the orange slice in her beer. "So, you don't have any evidence at all?"

Paula shook her head. "We went over every centimeter of everything. We were able to account for all the shoe print casts and fingerprints. We tested all the blood. Only the victim's."

"What about hair?" Cutty asked.

"Only the victim's." Paula looked up as their server put plates in front of them and a large pizza on a pedestal.

"Enjoy," the server said.

Paula didn't realize how hungry she was until the aromas of the sauce, cheese, and lots of roasted vegetables hit her nostrils. "Looks great."

They pulled off slices and munched for a while. Maybe Paula was just hungry, but she was pretty sure this was about the best pizza she'd ever had.

Cutty pulled a second slice to her plate, looked down at it, and then up at Paula. "I found a sliver of metal."

"I hope you're not talking about in the pizza," Paula said.

Cutty snorted and laughed. "The cave got flooded after all the stuff was removed. I went to have a look at it. I found the sliver under where the power cable had been cut."

Paula chewed a mouthful of pizza as she kept down a rising anticipation. "A piece of wiring?"

"Uh, no." Cutty took a sip of beer and gave Paula a speculative look. "So, what's the procedure for joining an investigation?"

Paula picked up a piece of green pepper off her slice and popped it into her mouth. "Are you using potential evidence as a bribe?"

Cutty wobbled her head. "Maybe." She squinted at Paula. "Do I need to use it as a bribe?"

Paula smiled as she munched another bite of pizza. "Can you get the time off?"

"You know, everyone around here is really anxious to know what happened in that cave," Cutty said. "I'm sure the county will let me go for a while. Especially if I can talk my grandfather into stepping out of retirement to keep things working smoothly."

"Your grandfather?"

"He was chief for forty years," Cutty said. "I used to spend my summers in Lipping Creek with my grandparents while my parents traveled to do their research. Then when I got out of school, I started working for grandpa and the people of Lipping Creek seemed to want to keep law enforcement in the family, so I got appointed chief when he retired."

"And he wouldn't mind?"

Cutty snorted a laugh. "You kidding? He still walks the town every day. He does more visiting than actual patrolling these days, but protecting Lipping Creek is something that's in his bones."

Paula rolled the glass of beer between her hands. "Well, the head of the repository has to approve all applications for archival access and research collaboration."

Cutty cocked her head. "Isn't that you?"

Paula tossed her head back and laughed. "I wish I could say that was a test for paying attention, but I'm not that clever."

Cutty grinned. "Believe it or not, not having much stuff to investigate helps the powers of observation. I play a game with my deputies by asking them what they see and what they think . . . It makes our jobs more interesting and keeps us sharp."

"If I approve your application with a handshake, will you tell me what you found?" Paula gave Cutty a sheepish look. "I admit I'm dying of curiosity."

Cutty held out her hand over the last slices of pizza. Paula gave it a good shake.

Cutty took a sip of beer and leaned forward. "It looks like a part of a blade."

Paula's breath caught in her throat. "Blade."

"Yep." Cutty popped that last bite of her slice into her mouth.

"Well, a piece of blade wouldn't be that unusual in a cave that's frequented by hikers, not to mention generations of indigenous people."

Cutty nodded. "I agree, but for a couple of things." She pulled another slice onto her plate.

"What do I have to agree to, to get that info out of you?"

Cutty shook with laughter. "You're lucky I'm just as anxious to tell someone as you're curious to hear it."

Paula held up her hand and took a healthy gulp of beer. "Okay. I'm ready."

Cutty pulled a stack of photos from her jacket pocket. She took the top one and handed it to Paula.

Paula studied the photo of something metal with sand stuck to it in a clear plastic bag next to a ruler. Four inches long and about two inches at its widest. She ran her finger over the image of the shiny, untarnished metal. The shape was an elongated rectangle with a long edge tapered to a point. Like a fragment of half the tip of a sizable blade.

"Okay, it doesn't look like a Swiss Army knife," she said.

"Or a camp knife," Cutty said.

"But you don't know how long it had been in the cave." Paula looked up.

"First off. The FBI did an amazing job of cleaning out the cave." Cutty shuffled through the photos and handed another one to Paula.

Paula took the photo. The cave wall, captured with a camera flash by the looks of it. A gash looked unnatural. She held it closer to her eyes.

Cutty held out another photo. Paula took it, catching Cutty's look of curiosity.

The photo was a close-up of the gash. The inside was chiseled smooth while the edges looked uneven and chipped.

"What's your theory?" She handed the photos back to Cutty.

"The perpetrator sliced the power cable with her sword—"

"I think it's interesting you feel the perp is female," Paula said.

"What bit of evidence we have points that way." Cutty shrugged. "Anyway, my theory is, she cut the power cable, and her sword got stuck in the wall, she struggled to free it, and this part broke off and stayed in the wall. It was still in the wall when the cave was cleaned out."

"And the FBI guys missed it?" Paula asked.

"I did some measuring. The gash was nine feet up. That kind of tells us something about the height of the perp, and I'm hoping this sliver can tell us the length of the blade." Cutty pulled off a piece of crust from the slice of pizza and chewed it. "It was deep enough in the gash that you'd have to shine a light on it just right to see it. So, it could have fallen out after the FBI left."

Paula put another slice of pizza on her plate and took a bite. Cutty nibbled on her own slice as she watched Paula with a look of curiosity and a hint of amusement.

Paula washed the pizza down with a swig of beer. "So, we're looking for a six-foot-tall woman with a sword that has a chink taken out of it." She nodded as if to herself. "I think Xena's retired."

"I think it's more like unemployed," Cutty said.

Paula cocked her head. She liked Cutty's spirit. "You know, you're right. This case has more evidence than I've found in any case in the whole repository."

"Must be a small repository."

Paula looked up at her, surprised, threw her head back and laughed. "You're going to fit right in."

PART II

Putting the Unusual in Unsolvable Crime

Chapter 6

CUTTY'S EARS WERE still popping as she stepped off the plane at Dulles airport. Her first time on a plane. She had a feeling this whole experience was going to be a series of firsts. Her legs felt both rubbery and like lead as she trudged down the long ramp, through the gate, and into the crowded, noisy waiting area. The cold air from the tunnel clashed uncomfortably with the overheated clusters of people in sweaters and winter coats. The too bright fluorescent lights added to the cacophony bombarding her senses.

She shuffled out of the way of the streams of travelers and found a corner between a pillar and the wall to stop. She took a deep breath, closed her eyes, and worked to recover her equilibrium. She had never realized flying affected the body and head so much.

"Okay, okay. Pull yourself together," she muttered. She hated to feel any kind of weakness, especially when everyone else around her seemed to be so unaffected by flying.

She adjusted her messenger-style computer bag and smoothed down her leather jacket and crew neck sweater. She stepped into the stream of travelers and allowed them to carry her past the security checkpoint. A crowd with eager, expectant faces was crammed into too small of an area in front of her, like spectators of a never-ending reality show. Many greeted and hugged the travelers surging around her. Her breath caught in her throat as panic washed over her. What if Paula forgot or had a breakdown or . . . ?

"Cutty." Paula, looking dorky, and Cutty had to admit, quite adorable in her wire-rims, baggy khakis, and shapeless orange turtleneck under a bright burgundy windbreaker, pushed awkwardly around the people greeting and hugging each other and waved at her.

Cutty laughed at her silliness and didn't feel nervous anymore. Why did she keep forgetting that no matter where she was, people were only human?

Paula trotted up to her. "Hey. Did you have a good flight?"

"Since my frame of reference is extremely narrow, it was a good flight."

"First time?"

"Yep."

"Well, now you get to experience waiting for your luggage," Paula said. "One of the great joys of air travel."

Cutty winnowed behind Paula through the crowd to the rows of huge conveyors. Twenty long minutes later, they pulled off her two suitcases on rollers and escaped the mayhem.

Cutty slapped her hands over her face as the sliding glass doors opened and the sunlight smacked her right in the eyes. "Whoa."

Paula stopped and waited for Cutty to blink away the whiteout.

"My eyes don't dilate properly. On the other hand, I can read in really low light and can see in near darkness." Cutty blinked through the white spots until her eyes stopped tearing.

"Maybe you should have been a scholarly cat." Paula led the way past a row of airport shuttles and across the street to a huge parking lot. "I got lucky and found a close spot."

They walked halfway down a line of cars with Virginia, DC, and Maryland license plates. They stopped behind a . . . Cutty blinked at it then stared at Paula, mystified.

Paula stopped lifting the trunk door and looked back at her with a puzzled expression.

"Uh." Cutty didn't quite know how to react to the . . . Well, it looked like an adult version of an erector set vehicle. Painted orange. Bright orange.

Paula grinned and pulled the trunk open, revealing a rubber-lined interior.

Cutty lifted her bags into a clear spot between a camp stove and a blue cooler. "I'm sure there's an interesting story behind this."

Paula laughed as she shut the trunk, stepped back, and patted the bumper with affection. "I built it on a dare."

Cutty took several steps back and stared at the vehicle. It looked as if a couple of drunken Bucky balls tried to dance the tango. "Uh, who won?"

Paula put her hands on her hips and gave her a "very funny" look.

Cutty laughed. "You built it?"

"Top to bottom, from stuff found at garage sales," Paula said.

"I take it, you don't mean mechanics' garages," Cutty said, amused.

"Nope." Paula hit a button on a key fob. The lights flashed, and Cutty heard the locks pop. "The kind your parents have."

Cutty shook her head in amazement as she went to the passenger door. At least she thought it was a door. It had a handle . . . of sorts. She cocked her head as she studied a long ridge of twisted metal. The door popped open, and she stepped back startled.

"The Bat Mobile in disguise?" she asked.

"My team calls it the Splatmobile," Paula said as she climbed into the driver's side.

Cutty stared at Paula, alarmed.

"Splat as in what would happen to anything that hit it." Paula patted the dashboard. "Built like a tank."

Cutty let out a held breath in relief and climbed in. She looked around at the interior, the color scheme a patchwork of various blues. Real car bucket seats, dashboard, gear shift, steering wheel . . . "You didn't get all this at a garage sale."

Paula shrugged. "Actually, it was more of a yard sale out in the country with the remains of an ancient VW bug next to all the stuff for sale. The owner let me pretty much strip it for a hundred bucks."

Cutty pulled on the seat belt and settled back. "Is that where you got the engine and stuff like that?"

Paula grinned and pushed a button where she'd normally insert a key.

Cutty frowned at the whine that came from where the engine should be.

Paula glanced at her. "I built the engine. It's electric. The only thing I couldn't get at garage sales were the batteries."

"Cool. How long did it take?" Cutty asked as Paula backed up the vehicle in an eerie silence. She was just getting used to electric vehicles tooling around.

"Two years." Paula navigated the long aisle of cars to the exit and through the pay booth.

She pulled onto a multi-laned road right out of the parking lot and much to Cutty's frustration kept following offshoots that steered away from the signs pointing to Washington DC. She knew she'd get to see the nation's capital soon enough, but they were so close she wished they could just follow those signs and do a quick tour around it.

The countryside wasn't too different from Southern Illinois, except more cultivated and populated. But the rolling hills made it familiar and comfortable. The traffic, on the other hand, was not making her comfortable at all.

"Two years to find everything and build it?" Cutty asked.

"Yep." Paula patted the steering wheel. "I built it in the garage of the house I lived in while I was in library school. Everything was spread out like a jigsaw puzzle, and I just started piecing it together and looked for stuff as I needed it. It was fun, mentally and physically challenging, and relaxing all at the same time."

"How many miles does it get on a charge?"

"Up to five-hundred miles, depending on the speed," Paula said. "The Interstate can chew up the charge."

Cutty frowned. "That's really good."

Paula gave her a sidelong look. "You really think the big car companies are going to release electric engines that can go the optimum? Not when the gas companies are still in charge."

Cutty turned to her. "Well, anyone who can collect stuff from garage sales and envision it all into a car sounds like the perfect person to solve unsolvable crimes."

"The difference is looking for known things or create known things out of known materials," Paula said. "But how does one find unknown things or create unknown things out of unknown materials?"

They rolled past several sprawling office complexes and then were surrounded by a forest, almost barren in the November chill.

"I believe as long as there's a piece then the whole puzzle can be put together," Cutty said.

Paula flashed an enigmatic look at her. "Wait until you see all the pieces."

Cutty frowned. "I thought I had."

Paula laughed. "This isn't the first crime involving a sword with no other evidence."

"Seriously?" Cutty gave her all her attention.

"I hope you like puzzles with ninety-nine percent of the pieces missing." Paula grinned as she took the off ramp to the Interstate.

CUTTY COULDN'T BELIEVE the size of the building that housed the unusual and unsolvable crimes. Paula said it used to be a warehouse hub for the major retail stores because the land was cheap and the Interstate was nearby. It had been abandoned for larger facilities. *Larger than this?*

She looked around the open room that overlooked the five-hundred-thousand square foot, three-story-high building. The room at one end overlooking the rest of the building was about halfway between the floor and the ceiling and had originally been offices. Paula and her staff of two had somehow turned the industrial cinder block walls and tangle of oversized pipes running on the ceiling into a space that was cozy and homey.

The main living section was like an open loft with an amazing chef's kitchen filled with shiny silver appliances and a seriously impressive pots and pans rack hanging over a butcher block island, a dining area with a heavy wood table and chairs, and a living room dominated by a huge flat screen television and comfy, lived-in-looking couches and chairs. Free-standing bookshelves of different sizes, filled with books, CDs, and magazines bookended nooks and crannies of tables and chairs and all kinds of knickknacks and tapestries that would do a flea market proud. Cutty smiled as she surveyed the room. It did look like a flea market, in the neatest, most wonderful sense. Windows lined the back wall, letting in what was left of the afternoon sun.

Doors to small bedrooms were on the lengthwise walls, enough for the three residents and several visitors. Paula had explained they sometimes felt a little isolated living in such a remote, rural area.

Her room had a futon with a comforter of autumn colors, a chest of drawers, and a couple of easy chairs and a desk and chair. One wall had built-in bookshelves. And actually half-filled with books—most looking like refugees from library and yard sales.

She filled the drawers with her clothes, put her laptop on the desk, and stood in the middle of the room. She had thought she was tired and needed a nap, but now that she was here, she wanted nothing more than to dive into the mystery.

"I can sleep later." She gave herself a resolved nod.

She pulled on a hoodie—the warehouse was drafty—and walked out of the room. She detected the smell of yeast and detoured to the kitchen. She followed her nose around a long island lined with a bar and stools to an industrial-sized bowl covered with an overlapping pair of dish towels.

She lifted an edge of the cloth. A beautiful dough was rising.

A large silver pot with a flat lid sat on the stove. She lifted the lid and a steam of tomato sauce misted her face.

"Hmmm. Can't wait for dinner."

She went to the balcony that overlooked the enormous warehouse. It was sectioned into what looked like remnants of freestanding shelving and wall panels from when it had been a distribution center, creating several humongous rooms and a bunch of smaller ones that most people would consider good sized. She guessed it was all a matter of perspective. The huge rooms really did look like the last scene from *Raiders of the Lost Ark*.

She gazed into the one directly below her at the row upon row of crates and file boxes and furniture and equipment and haphazard piles of stuff—musty, dusty, old, and neglected for decades. They must have piled everything on trucks and moved it, dirt, dust, and all, to this new place. All of it potential evidence for unusual and unsolvable crimes. No wonder Paula laughed at her small facility comment.

She trotted down the metal steps that switched back to the wide center corridor. She grinned at the gaudy skateboards propped against the wall. A bullseye with blue, white, and red bands was painted in the middle of the corridor. She inspected it closer and realized it was for curling. Lines intersected the bullseye and ran further down the corridor to another bullseye. Along the sides of the curling area were long lines of the colors of the rainbow. She walked along one side, studying the lines, wondering if they looked like the rainbow flag on purpose. That would be a welcomed surprise.

"I guess the big bosses never visit." She walked past a break in the wall partitions to one of the ultra-huge rooms, then stopped, backed up, and peeked inside. Her nose twitched at the mingled scents of mildew and dust. "*Raiders of the Lost Ark* on steroids."

She refused to let her mind be boggled by the enormity of all the space and too much stuff ever to get archived and put in order. She was there to solve just one crime. Well, maybe more, but that would only be a by-product of solving her specific crime.

Okay, quit getting ahead of yourself and go find Paula.

She ignored all the rooms and headed toward the music. Lady Gaga. The previous song had been James Taylor, and earlier, Michael Jackson, Queen Latifah, Brandi Carlile, and the Indigo Girls. Like musical confetti. Maybe she could add her Shawn Colvin and Antje D. to the mix.

She passed a partition that had a mural of what looked like mythical beasts sketched out and partially painted. The music was coming from the other side of the partition.

She peeked around the flimsy wall and then stepped inside. A long roll of white paper with a color-coded timeline carefully drawn on it was duct taped to the cinder block wall. A half-dozen white boards filled with equally colorful writing and drawings stood around the periphery. Several long work tables covered with papers, files, and books occupied the middle of the chamber. Open file boxes were scattered around. Two very well-worn but comfortable-looking couches sat in front of the corridor partition and faced all this stuff. A fluffy gray and white cat was curled up on a pillow on one of the couches.

Paula, perched on a stool, looked up from studying something on the table, pushed up her glasses, and grinned. "Come in, come in." She gestured Cutty in—her enthusiasm almost comical.

A tall, slim young woman looked around from behind one of the white boards.

"This is Brie." Paula waved at Brie. "Our cryptic expert."

Brie bounced across the room and playfully whopped Paula on the arm. "She always does that. I'm an expert in cryptology."

Cutty smiled as she walked to the work table. "Which doesn't necessarily mean you're not cryptic."

Brie dramatically grabbed her head with both hands. "Not another one. I want a transfer," she wailed, then grinned and held out her hand. "Nice to meet you, Cutty. Sanity is optional here and not necessarily a desirable trait."

"Nice to meet you." Cutty shook Brie's hand.

"The third member of our motley crew has gone into town—" Paula began.

"Meaning Marshall," Brie put in.

"—to get some interesting food type supplies," Paula said. "He's good at analyzing data, but more importantly, he trained to be a chef before he went to library school."

"I smelled the dough in the kitchen," Cutty said.

Brie did a Snoopy happy dance. "Get ready for the world's greatest pizza."

"He even has a special vegetarian one," Paula said.

"Wow. Can't wait." Cutty gazed around the room.

"Welcome to ground zero for one of the greatest mysteries no one knows about." Paula spread out her arms and spun around.

Cutty focused on several books opened to pages with illustrations of swords. "My mystery?"

Paula sauntered to the beginning of the timeline. "One and the same."

"Wow." Cutty followed Paula to the wall.

Above each section in the timeline was a neat line by line entry of data. The precise organization was impressive.

She took a closer look at the first date. And then a second look. "BCE?"

"Yep." Paula nodded as she gazed at the timeline with pride. "We can thank Mr. Frederick Manning, the first director of the RUUC, for all this research. He became obsessed with the unsolved sword crimes, and consequently, uncovered all this."

Cutty felt like she'd walked onto the set of a blockbuster adventure movie. "Where did he even find all this information?"

Brie chuckled. "That's what we've been wondering. The archives had like zero budget for real research back then."

"He filled dozens of journals with notes on his research, but certain information, like his sources are written in some kind of code or ancient language," Paula said.

"Whatever the code is, he had to have made it up," Brie said. "I haven't been able to find the key yet."

Cutty walked down the timeline. Ancient, ancient murders. Sketches of swords—all very much the same. Sketches of the fatal wound—all very much the same. "He was a researcher and an archivist. He wouldn't intentionally hide information forever. Just hide it away from everyone but the people really serious about these crimes."

"Well, we're serious and we're going to break his code," Paula said. "In the meantime, we have all this to work with."

Cutty raised an eyebrow. "And where does it all go?"

Paula sighed and ran a hand through her hair. "Somewhere, I hope."

Chapter 7

PAULA WANDERED BETWEEN the towers of crates and boxes. She flashed her flashlight beam over the yellowed wood and acid-free white file boxes. She wanted to know what was in all those boxes. How did so many crimes be deemed unusual or unsolvable?

They had entered the basic details of all the crimes into a database, but that had only excited her curiosity and desire to solve them. She had to keep telling herself that their job was to simply catalog the evidence and documentation for future researchers of the soon to be built public Archives and Museum of Unusual Unsolvable Crimes. Fortunately, the Smythe Foundation was now overseen by Seymour Richard's granddaughter, Marion Smythe, who was obsessed with frozen cases—cases so cold they were hard as ice to break—and provided a very generous allowance for them to be as thorough as possible in their research for what she called feature crimes that would bring tourists and researchers to the museum.

What better crowd-pleaser than the series of unsolved murders involving a sword?

She went down the end of the aisle and followed the cinder block wall to where all of Mr. Manning's items had been piled. Somewhere in these haphazard stacks of stuff was the key to his code. It had to be there.

She went past cobwebbed boxes and dust-covered crates of household and office objects that represented every decade since the 1920s to the end where Mr. Manning's heavy oak office furniture was heaped.

"Okay, one piece at a time." She lifted a captain's chair and examined it. Would he have put it on a piece of furniture?

She put down the chair and tried to think through the logic. He would have assumed his furniture would be re-assigned or even thrown out, given the usual office practice. He would not have considered a zero budget for new equipment for his successor. And when the repository was moved to this facility, they moved everything because of the lack of budget for a lot of new stuff.

Nothing had been thrown out, and she was thankful she had perfected the art of yard-saling and browsing Goodwill and thrift shops. Not to mention building things from odds and ends.

"So where would he hide a code?"

She stepped back and studied the jumbled stacks of yellowing books and file folders and the red marbled leather binding on a lot of journals peeking out from under everything.

She was sure she had all the sword journals because they had been carefully packed in two file boxes. But what if he had more information about the sword crimes in other journals?

"Okay." She found a journal near the top that she could easily remove. "Start with the journals."

CUTTY OPENED HER eyes. Eggs and toast. She tried to roll over to look at the clock on the nightstand and ran into something soft and solid at the same time. She looked over the edge of the comforter pooling around her neck. A huge, short-haired tabby with beautiful orange fur was curled up against her.

"Now I know who usually sleeps in this bed."

She shifted so she didn't disturb the cat and looked at the clock. Six-thirty. Five-thirty, central time. A folding tray holding a domed platter stood next to the bed.

"I don't remember ordering breakfast in bed."

Jeff had asked what she liked for breakfast, down to how she liked her eggs, but she figured it had been for future grocery runs.

She pulled herself up, and the cat sleepily opened its eyes and blinked at her. It stretched and climbed to its feet and moved down to the foot of the bed, curled up, and was most likely asleep in seconds.

She dangled her legs over the edge of the bed and lifted the dome, releasing a cloud of aromas. Two fried eggs, wheat toast, what smelled like blueberry marmalade, apple juice. She sniffed the over-sized latte mug. Soy chai. Paula had to have told him that was her favorite form of caffeine before he went shopping.

She got up and wrapped her arms around herself, then pulled on a baggy sweatshirt. It was cooler in Virginia than in Southern Illinois. Made sense, Virginia was farther north. She picked up the platter, went to the desk, and powered up her laptop.

She got back from the funky bathroom to find all her email had downloaded. Not anything she needed to attend to right away. She logged onto the Licking Creek police department cloud and brought up the feeds from the cameras in the cave.

So far, the action activated cameras had caught a couple of raccoons and a bobcat investigating the cave and a few hikers. The cameras were a long shot but she would have kicked herself if she hadn't covered all the possible bases.

The eggs were perfectly cooked, and the bread tasted freshly baked. She could get used to this kind of room service.

"Knock, knock." Paula poked her head around the open doorway.

Cutty looked up. "Come on in. Just checking my mail and the cave surveillance."

Paula, dressed in sweats, t-shirt, and an oversized terry cloth robe, walked in and scratched the cat behind the ear.

"This is Mac's room, but he's pretty amiable about sharing," she said.

"He's a great hot water bottle." Cutty grinned at the purring cat.

"That'll become a greater asset as we get further into November." Paula patted Mac's head and walked to Cutty. "Did you sleep well?"

"Like a log," Cutty said.

"Good." Paula nodded. "I'm not much of a sleeper. Genetic insomnia. So don't be alarmed if I nod off at odd times."

"Is this breakfast in bed a welcome to the team thing?" Cutty picked up the latte mug and took a sip.

"No, no." Paula crossed her arms and plopped down on the rocking chair. "He does that every morning if you don't get up before he does."

"What time does he get up?" Cutty asked.

Paula shrugged. "I'm never up that early to know."

Cutty turned her chair around to face Paula. "So you don't have a time clock here?"

Paula laughed. "We work when our minds are working and play when they're not. The funny thing is, we put in many more hours of work than if we were supervised or had to punch a time clock."

"That's because you have a fun job where you're surrounded by unsolved mysteries," Cutty said.

"Only fun for us crazy people who love the challenge of a good mystery and have no life or what most people would call a normal life." Paula patted both knees and stood up. "Well, I'd better hit the shower and get ready for another day of following the sword."

Cutty laughed. "Just save some hot water for me."

Paula paused in the doorway. "No worries about that. I rigged a redundant green power system with instant hot water."

"You can always go into green technologies if this archivist thing doesn't work out for you," Cutty said.

"Blame it on my eco-progressive parents," Paula said.

"And you're not a vegan?" Cutty asked.

"Yuppie-ish eco-progressive parents." Paula gave her a wry grin. "Don't pollute the world, but don't take away their hamburgers either."

Cutty laughed. "I grew up around academia, so I know exactly the type."

"Yep," Paula said. "Professor's kid. My father, not surprisingly, teaches engineering."

"My mother teaches biochemistry and my father, viola," Cutty said.

"Must make for interesting dinnertime talk." Paula grinned and waggled her fingers as she walked out of the room.

Chuckling, Cutty turned back to her laptop. She pulled up her email and deleted all the spam. She *wished* she had won the Italian lottery. She read through the emails from her parents and wrote back, promising a more detailed description of this unusual place when she had the time.

She clicked on the email from Jen with the subject line, "Squeeeelll." Her trusty deputy was going to see The Black Warriors perform in St. Louis. Jen had been bopping to the group's music all summer. They had a hit song, "Slay Me," that played constantly on the radio.

A publicity photo of the group displayed below Jen's gushing, excited text. Hmmm. Four very fit-looking strong women, staring at the camera with calm, intelligent eyes. This was not some gushy pop group.

They didn't look American. Their complexion was too fair. She seemed to recall that they were from Ireland or Scotland. The black and red hair, fair skin, and deep blue and green eyes backed up this memory.

Good for Jen for scoring tickets to see them in person. Going to a concert in St. Louis meant crashing in a downtown hotel and unwinding with friends, plus eating at the Spaghetti Factory in the warehouse district. They all needed a big city fix every once in a while.

She gazed at the photo. "Looks like an interesting group of women."

Chapter 8

PAULA PUSHED A clean whiteboard into the sword room. Time for serious focus and brainstorming. She roamed around the room, nervous they didn't really have any clues that could lead to something concrete they could follow.

"We're going to run out of things to talk about after five minutes." She sighed as she put colored markers on the whiteboard's tray. Was she just swinging at windmills? Did Cutty disrupt her job and her life for nothing?

Crazy laughter and running echoed through the building.

Jeff ran past the opening between partitions. Brie sauntered into the sword room. Cutty walked to the opening and stood with hands on her hips, giving them a look.

"I've seen curling on TV," she said. "Shuffleboard on ice."

"More like chess on ice," Jeff said as he scooted past her into the room.

Cutty shook her head and followed Jeff.

Paula pushed down her doubts and grinned. "I foresee a curling tournament in your future."

Cutty turned to Jeff and Brie. "I look forward to it."

Jeff grinned. "Cool."

"You just want to add another convert to your cult of curling." Paula crossed her arms.

"All a part of my nefarious plan to take over the world and promote world peace through curling." Jeff plopped down on one of the couches.

Paula shook her head and pushed the whiteboard in front the couch. Cutty and Brie sat on either side of Jeff.

"Ready, boss," Brie said.

They looked up at her with eager and expectant eyes. As if she was going to channel the gods of evidence and pull important tidbits out of the air.

"The best place to start is to list what we know and then brainstorm ideas on how to find what we don't have." Paula gave them a hopeful look and was bolstered by their amiable nods.

"We have a piece of a sword," Brie said.

Paula nodded as she picked up the blue marker and wrote "Evidence" at the top left of the whiteboard. Beneath it she wrote "sword piece."

"That's the one thing we have that none of the other sword cases have," Jeff said.

"And . . ." Paula went to a work table and picked up her pad of paper. "I did a lot of research on ancient metals and did some testing that didn't harm the fragment. This metal is consistent with steel smelted about twenty-five hundred years ago."

Her audience stared at her stunned and wide-eyed.

"Seriously?" Brie asked.

"Yeah. But it could also be an excellent replica of the ancient steel." Paula flipped over a few pages on her pad. "Here's what I found out so far about twenty-five-hundred-year-old swords. Making steel back then was akin to magic. Swordsmiths were considered wizards. Steel was extremely hard to make and even harder to fashion into a sword. A village might have only one or two steel swords and warlords would raid villages just to collect these swords for their armies."

"And someone has one of these swords?" Cutty pushed her hands through her hair. "To use as a murder weapon. Wouldn't a sword that old be, well, too old?"

"It's steel and, if it's really that old, it seems to be very well preserved." Paula held up a finger. "But it did break off when it got stuck in the wall."

"There can't be many of those swords left." Brie leaned forward and grabbed a handful of popcorn from the full oversized bowl on the coffee table. They joked that most of their budget went to popcorn, chips, and other munchable junk food.

"I've sent what we know about the sword to several experts," Paula said. "Hopefully, they'll be able to shed some light on this particular one."

"What else do we have?" Jeff popped a piece of popcorn into his mouth and chewed.

Paula sighed. "We have a dead body."

Cutty got up and walked around the coffee table to the whiteboard. "We have what Mr. Jones was doing in the cave."

"Okay." Paula clasped her hands together. "What was he doing?"

"He had a lot of International government and defense data on those servers," Brie said. "And not taken off of Wikipedia. He seems to have hacked into departmental servers."

"He had been a government systems analyst." Cutty picked up a green marker and started a category called "Harvey Jones" and wrote "government systems analyst" next to "sword piece." She stood back and gazed at the two phrases. "Only one answer. Time travel."

Jeff rubbed his chin. "Ya know, that still would raise a lot of questions. For instance, it would have to be time and distance travel. The sword is most likely a Celtic broadsword, popular in what is now Europe. The perp would have had to travel either the distance first or time travel first and get here. I don't think she would have been able to get on a plane without a photo ID, even if she checked the sword in as luggage. On the other hand, she could have traveled the distance first and then time traveled . . ."

"Okay." Paula picked up the red pen and created the "other theories" category and wrote beneath it "time travel." "Why would a woman warrior belonging to a Celtic tribe in 500 BCE Europe want to stop an American twenty-first century former government systems analyst?"

They stared at the words on the board.

As weird as it sounded, Paula could feel a connection between these words that looked more like the premise for a science fiction novel. A connection that danced just on the edge of her imagination.

CUTTY STARED AT the oversized piping on the ceiling. She had spent three days spinning theories and going through files of unsolved sword crimes that had occurred since the Justice Department started collecting them. Looking for differences, similarities, things the other crimes didn't have . . . Three days of learning enough about these crimes to be an expert on them. Expert on everything except solving them.

She looked at the clock on the nightstand. 11:45.

"Maybe if I walk around a bit . . ."

She scratched Mac's neck before easing out from under the comforter. Mac sleepily expanded into the space she had occupied. She laughed. She wished she could relax like a cat who trusted its surroundings.

She shivered and slipped on her fuzzy slippers and a baggy sweatshirt. She went to her partially opened door—she had been told that Mac would keep her awake half the night if he couldn't get in and out of the room when he wanted to.

The common room was quiet, peaceful, comfortable. Amazing what a little creative TLC could do. She squinted at the dark masses on the sofa and chairs. Some of Mac's friends. She was slowly learning all their names and personalities.

She went to the balcony that expanded the width of the warehouse. Only the emergency lights were on. A flash illuminated the far wall. She frowned and concentrated on the area. She maybe saw another flash, but her eyes could be playing tricks or she'd seen too many *Ghost Hunter* episodes. *Scritch*. What was that? Sounded like it came from where the flashes were. She stared at the wall and opened up her hearing. More noise. She knew no one could get into the building. The heavy-duty security system had been reinforced by some low-tech and very entertaining enhancements by the ever-resourceful staff.

Scraping. Sounded like furniture being moved. She doubted the cats were that industrious. Paula had mentioned that she liked to rummage when her insomnia flared.

"Sounds like insomnia-induced rummaging to me."

She trotted down the stairs, her slippered feet leaving soft footfalls on the metal steps. She walked down the long central corridor, peeking into the shadowed Bays. The place seemed a lot bigger in the dimmed safety lighting. Not spooky. Rather appealing, like the gray of twilight. A time of impermanent stillness. She felt more comfort in the gray light than in the night blackness or clear, sunny day. "Laughter is day, and sobriety is night; a smile is the twilight that hovers gently between both, more bewitching than either." Henry Beecher Ward. Poetic words from a preacher and abolitionist she made an effort to memorize because she never wanted to forget them.

She slipped into the Bay where she had seen the flash. The crates towered upward of ten to fifteen feet on either side of the aisle as she shuffled on the polished floor. Dark monolithic towers of mystery. God. She would love to dive into every one of those crates and solve the crime.

"Okay. Let me guess." Paula's voice came from near the wall. "It has to be Cutty."

Cutty smiled as she approached the end of the aisle. Paula was a few feet away with her hands on her hips, studying a pile of stuff.

"Let me guess." Cutty looked down at her feet. "My bushy slippers gave me away."

Paula turned to her and winked. "Brie likes to do Xena battle yells and Jeff can't be quiet to save his life. Let's just say, he would flunk sneaking around in FBI training school."

Cutty snorted a laugh as she looked at the pile of stuff next to the wall. "What is all this?"

"This"—Paula waved a hand—"is the personal property of Frederick Manning, the person who headed this archive for forty-two years."

"Why didn't he take his stuff when he retired?" Cutty picked up a wooden bookend carved in the shape of a book.

"Because he retired on the job, so to speak," Paula said.

Cutty looked at her, confused.

"He died at his desk." Paula shrugged. "His successor didn't do any work, as far as I can tell, except file new crimes and cash paychecks. Manning's stuff got packed up with everything else when the division was moved to this facility. It got dumped here because it didn't fit anywhere else."

"So you're looking for the key to his code?" Cutty asked.

"Yep." Paula pulled a journal from under a glass paperweight. "At least you can use a magnet with a haystack."

Cutty bit her bottom lip as she studied the remnants of a man's life. "Well, if you wanted to hide a code that you wanted to be found. Where would you put it?"

Paula frowned. "Well, putting it that way . . . I'd put it somewhere that wouldn't be disposed of or re-used or re-assigned."

"So, he wouldn't have etched it on the bottom of the desk or put it in the hollow leg of a chair, or in a hidden drawer in any kind of furniture," Cutty said.

"It doesn't make much sense that he'd write it in one of his other journals." Paula scratched her head.

"Beale papers." Cutty's mind caught fire at the idea. "A book cipher."

"What document would he choose?" Paula also looked intrigued.

"It makes sense he'd pick something related to these sword crimes," Cutty said.

Paula sighed as she tossed the journal on a stack of books. "It's not like there's a declaration of criminal activity involving swords . . ." She blinked and held up a finger.

Cutty waited as Paula processed her idea.

"Is it possible?" Paula muttered as she turned and walk-ran down an aisle.

Cutty trotted-slid after her. "What?"

"Just a hunch." Paula ran out of the Bay and down the corridor.

Cutty slipped-shuffled after her.

Paula skidded into the sword room. Cutty slid to the opening and took in the sight of Paula dragging file boxes away from the wall.

She sauntered up to her. "Are you looking for something? Or just possessed with the sudden need to re-arrange boxes?"

Paula looked up at her. "Sarcasm isn't allowed in the Justice Department, even in the archives of Justice Department stuff. Most agents don't have a sarcasm detection gene and digital sarcasm detectors aren't standard issue."

Cutty spluttered a laugh and looked around. "Shhh. This place may be bugged."

"Nah." Paula flashed her a grin. "If that were true, we'd be selling shaved ice on a California beach for a living by now."

Cutty crossed her arms and gave Paula a speculative look. "If you hold the Justice Department in such disdain. Why did you become an archivist for their stuff?"

Paula straightened and cocked her head. "Seriously?"

"Yeah," Cutty said. "If that's possible for you."

Paula chuckled. "I like doing this kind of research. I mean *this* kind of research." She pointed her index fingers at the floor. "I wanted to work in these archives the moment I learned they existed while I was in library school."

"Did you work here before you became the head honcho?" Cutty asked.

Paula shook her head. "I was an archivist at the National Archive of Criminal Justice Data at the University of Michigan when I applied for the job, which really wasn't enough to get me a head honcho job but two circumstances converged. The first, I also have a Ph.D. in history and my dissertation was on the great unsolved crimes in history, so I had demonstrated an interest in the subject."

Cutty held up a finger. "Here comes the twist."

Paula gave her an impish grin. "Second, no one who was even remotely qualified applied for the job."

Cutty laughed. "You're kidding?"

"Seriously." Paula held out her arms. "Why wouldn't any archivist want to work in a warehouse the size of eight-and-a-half football fields filled with millions of pieces of evidence and files of unsolved crimes out in the middle of nowhere Virginia. I mean, what's the matter with these people?"

Cutty shook with laughter. "They got lucky you wanted the job, in other words."

"I like to think of it as karma." Paula looked up and around. "This is what I was meant to do."

"And Brie and Jeff . . . were they here already?"

Paula shook her head. "The whole staff resigned as soon as they realized a new boss meant actual work."

"Why didn't any of them apply for the job?"

"Because they weren't archivists," Paula said. "Brie and Jeff were the cream of the applications I got."

"Brilliant misfits." Cutty cocked her head. "Who also happen to represent the rainbow."

"You got it. We take pride in our work." Paula grinned as she shoved a few boxes out of the way. "Found it." She picked up a box, carried it to a work table, and sat on a stool.

"Case files?" Cutty pulled up on the stool next to Paula.

"No. This is the first file Mr. Manning writes about in his sword journals." Paula thumbed through the folders and pulled one out. She opened it and removed several sheets encased in plastic and spread them out on the table.

Cutty studied the sheets. A case report for a crime committed in 1922 in Columbus, Ohio. The paper was yellow-brown and brittle beneath the plastic sleeve. "This is your Declaration of Independence?"

"Take a closer look."

Cutty raised an eyebrow and picked up the first sheet. Old-fashioned report done on a typewriter with uneven key strikes . . . "What are these faint marks?" She held the sheet closer to her eyes. "Light pencil marks under random letters." She turned to Paula. "You think?"

"It'd be a real waste of coincidence if it isn't," Paula said.

Cutty sat back. "Looks like Brie's going to do a happy dance tomorrow."

Chapter 9

PAULA'S SIDES STILL ached from laughing at Brie's happy dance. How'd she get so lucky to have a staff who loved their job so much?

She turned at the sound of the mail cart on the move. Her mother said she had shipped her a couple of batches of her famous homemade whoopie pies. They'd be a great addition to the curling tournament they were holding that night. It was Friday night, after all.

The cart sped up with accompanying footfalls and then the footfalls stopped but the cart kept rolling with a more ungainly sounding gait.

Paula shook her head, amused. They were all big kids at heart. Thank god. She couldn't stand working with people who took themselves and their adulthood too seriously. She glanced at Cutty who was sprawled on the couch reading through a stack of files on the floor. What were the odds of finding a kindred spirit in the form of a police chief from a village in the middle of a national forest? Not to mention a cute-in-an-impish-sort-of-way police chief.

The mail cart passed the bay opening with Jeff, feet on the wheel brace, clinging to the back of it.

Cutty, facing the opening, lifted her head. "Hope those packages are insured."

"I think I caught a glimpse of my mother's gift wrap," Paula said. "Her whoopie pies can take the abuse."

Cutty grinned. "Sounds like there should be a hockey puck joke somewhere."

"Nope." Paula shook her head. "They're light and moist and as close to enlightenment as you can get without sitting under a tree for a week."

Cutty looked intrigued. "I hope you share."

"Are you kidding?" Paula grinned. "I'd have to lock them up to keep them away from the scavengers."

Cutty laughed as Jeff wheeled the mail cart into the bay.

"Fun stuff today." He picked up two boxes with flowery wrapping paper. "Our supplier has sent our whoopie pie fix."

Paula went up to him and took the boxes from his hands. "Not until the tournament tonight."

"Ahhh, mom." Jeff sighed and pulled a manilla envelope from the pile. "And then there's this intriguing little item from a Dr. Grayson Godersen."

Paula put her mom's packages on the table and took the envelope from Jeff. "Okay. Let's hope he has something interesting—"

"And useful," Cutty put in.

"—to tell us."

Paula took out her pocket knife, slit open the envelope, and pulled out several sheets. Top sheet, polite letter. Second sheet . . . she squinted at the boxes and rows of numbers and letters, plus techno-speak in pseudo-English . . . She held the sheet closer to her eyes . . . Maybe even some Elven. "Science-looking stuff." She handed the sheet to Jeff.

He grabbed it and eagerly scanned it.

"This looks like it's in English." Paula studied the last sheet.

"What does the letter say?" Cutty asked.

Paula handed her the letter and returned to scanning what looked like a summary of the sword fragment but felt more like a study in avoiding talking about the sword fragment. She frowned as she read through it again. "What exactly is he saying here?"

Cutty looked up from reading the letter. "Here he's saying that he can't say anything about the sword such a fragment may have come from."

"In a very loquacious manner, with scientific mumbo jumbo to back up everything he can't—or won't—tell us," Jeff said. "I'm leaning toward won't. He analyzed our metal analysis and basically says that our sword fragment couldn't possibly be made up of the material in the analysis. He also says the markings don't indicate anything and we shouldn't take it as an ancient example of pattern-welding."

"The letter says that the fragment couldn't have come from a sword and looks like a possible modern attempt to replicate ancient metallurgy," Cutty said.

Paula held up a finger. Something sparked on the edges of her mind. Something . . . odd. "Why would we even think it was something other than a replica of an old sword? I mean, we certainly wouldn't think it was from an actual ancient sword. We looked at photos of ancient steel swords. They're in pretty bad condition."

Cutty and Jeff gazed at her, expectant.

"I mean, why doesn't he just say it's from a modern replica of a sword?" Paula waved the summary at them. "This is protesting too much. And he probably thinks we'll accept whatever he says because he's an expert."

"Are you suggesting this fragment is what he's insisting it's not? That"—Cutty put her finger on the letter—"'it's not possible for this sword to be of the age the metal analysis suggests and it would be a waste of your time to pursue that line of inquiry.' And this is even better." She moved her finger to the next paragraph. "'Given my knowledge of the sword market, finding a sword that matches this fragment would be impossible.'" She tsked-tsked. "Dangling participle." She focused again on the text. "'It's my recommendation that you'd be wasting your time on this fragment as any kind of evidence in a crime.'" She looked up. "When someone tells me twice that something's a waste of my time, I'm twice as challenged to jump in and prove that person wrong."

Paula rubbed her chin. "So, we're dealing with a really old sword that has an expert trying to wipe away its existence."

"That's what it looks like to me," Cutty said.

"Me, too." Jeff pointed at the hieroglyphs in his page. "Here, he goes into extreme detail about why this analysis is actually something else. That it's impossible for any blade to have steel with that composition."

Paula sucked in a long breath and let it out slowly. "Okay. I guess we wait and see what everyone else we sent this to says. In the meantime, I think we ought to do some independent research on this kind of steel."

"Sounds like awesome fun," Jeff said.

"Remember, you're just researching steel in general." Paula paused. "How about, you're researching the ancient technique of steel making. This expert seems to be quite adamant about us not thinking this is from a really old sword, so we don't want to arouse suspicion."

"Even more awesome." Jeff turned the mail cart around. "I'll toss the rest of the mail in your rooms and start snooping." He pushed the cart out and ran it down the corridor.

Paula gathered up the sheets and put them back into the envelope. "Okay. We start a new folder for this stuff."

Cutty laughed as she pulled a file folder from a box next to the work table. "What should we call it? Evasive experts."

"Sounds good to me." Paula gave Cutty a speculative look. "What do you think? If we were dealing with a really ancient sword, why would an expert go to extremes to insist that it's not?"

Cutty wrote "Evasive Experts" on the file folder, put the pen down, and crossed her arms. "It sounds to me like he knows the sword. The exact sword."

Paula gazed at her as the idea seeped in. "Why else? Unless there's something special about a sword with this metallic composition."

"If it's an ancient sword, no two swords would have the same composition and the same etched pattern," Cutty said.

"So it has to be a known sword," Paula said. "And instead of saying so and being concerned that it may have been stolen and used to commit a crime, this expert is trying to divert us away from it."

"I wonder if Mr. Manning figured out the sword," Cutty said.

Paula bit her lip and shook her head. "He never had a piece of it for analysis."

"But he seems to know stuff that he felt he had to put in code," Cutty said.

Paula threw up her hands. "If it's Excalibur, I'm not jumping into a lake to look for it."

TOO MUCH PIZZA. Too much beer. Too many whoopie pies. Really, really good whoopie pies. And a humiliating defeat at warehouse curling . . . All in all, a fun night. Cutty rolled over and squinted at the clock. Nine o'clock.

Time to get up. She grabbed a sweatshirt, went to the desk, and powered up her laptop.

"Wonder how the concert went last night." She sat down and brought up her email. She clicked on the message from Jen. She laughed at all the exclamation marks. Jen said The Black Warriors concert was awesomely amazing. She certainly took a lot of photos. She even got some of the band leaving the arena. Cutty grinned. She was glad Jen got a chance to let loose.

She read through the email from her parents. They thought it was seriously cool she was working on an unsolved FBI case. Of course, being academics, all new experiences were seriously cool to them. They kept asking if she'd met Mulder and Scully yet.

"At least their weird mysteries were solvable."

Jen must have gone to the cave before she took off for the big city. New footage was on the cloud from the cameras. She fast forwarded all three feeds at the same time.

The crime had happened a month ago. How much longer should she monitor the cave?

A light flickered on in the cave. She stopped the feeds. Hikers. With a strong and bright flashlight. Not something most hikers carried, unless they were going to explore one of the many caves in the national forest. Looked like a woman with short dark spiky hair. Cutty squinted at the screen. Most hikers didn't wear black leather jackets, black t-shirts with some kind of design on them tucked into black jeans. The woman looked in the direction of the camera.

Whoa. Cutty stared into the most compelling eyes—she couldn't tell if they were blue or green—just glistening jewels reflecting the light. Her skin had a Northern European complexion, smooth white with cheeks reddened most likely from the cold weather. Even lit by flashlight, she had a presence.

The woman flashed the light onto the wall, illuminating the indentation. Cutty sat up. The woman held the light steady as she stood on her tiptoes to get a better look at the indentation. She seemed to be pretty tall.

The woman pulled something from her pocket. What was she doing? Cutty squinted as she tried to catch the chaotic movement of light as she used the hand with the flashlight to pull something long and gray from the other hand. She thought she saw flashes of metal. The woman stopped what she was doing and pointed the light at an indentation again and poked it with the gray thing.

"What the . . . ?" Cutty scrunched her nose. "Oh, a collapsible pointer. Not basic hiking equipment. That's for sure."

Cutty looked from feed to feed to see the woman from all angles.

The woman's expression turned curious and a bit panicked. She collapsed the pointer and ran the beam of her flashlight around the ground at the base of the wall. She got down on her knees and dug through the sand, going through the same patches several times. She finally sat back on her heels and gave the ground a blank, bleak look.

Cutty could tell she was fighting a rising panic, a rising realization that . . . She sucked in her breath. That a piece of her precious ancient sword was gone.

Cutty stared at her in stunned fascination. Did the experts know who owned the sword? Could they identify this woman? That certainly would cause panic . . . Wait. Why did she look familiar? Like really recent familiar. Who had she even seen recently outside this building? This woman certainly couldn't be one of the locals. That would be some kind of truly weird coincidence.

She shook her head to clear the fuzziness of sleep and remnants of the night-before beer haze. The woman stood and focused the flashlight on the incision in the wall again. She stared at the spot for a long time, as if not believing what she was looking for wasn't there. She flicked the light on her watch, then flashed it over the ground below the incision. After a moment's hesitation, she turned and strode out of the cave.

Cutty stopped the feed from the camera next to the cavern entrance and studied the woman's face. Those jewel-like eyes had a stricken expression in them. Stricken. Like she had lost all hope.

She did a screen capture of the face.

"Is she really our murderer?"

She sent the photo to the main printer in the sword room.

"Okay, take a deep breath. Take a shower, grab some tea and breakfast." She worked to remain calm. "Think it through."

She reduced the camera windows, revealing Jen's concert photos. She blinked and then stared in disbelief at a photo Jen had snapped of one of the band members as she was exiting the arena's back door. A striking woman with a strong angular face and fair skin and black spiky hair. Very Irish looking. She couldn't tell the eye color. The woman was tall and lean, yet strong looking, like she was made of muscle. She had on a black leather jacket and a black t-shirt and black jeans.

She saved the photo to the hard drive and sent it to the printer.

"Okay. Shower. Get some caffeine and any pre-made portable food." She grabbed the edge of the desk as she pushed down her mounting excitement. "A quick shower. Very quick shower." She jumped up and ran for the door.

Chapter 10

PAULA FROWNED AS the printer on the table in the corner came to life. She went to it and picked up an almost over-exposed photo of a woman with black spiky hair.

She shrugged, put the photo in the basket next to the printer, and went back to her laptop and her research on ancient swords.

The printer rumbled and churned. Paula looked up. Another photo. Overcome with curiosity, she went back to the printer and picked up the photo. She frowned and held it next to the other photo. She took both to a work table and sank down on a stool as she studied them. They looked like the same person.

"Who sent . . . ?"

She blinked at the garish photo. Yes. Had to be the cameras in the cave. Cutty caught someone.

She slipped off the stool and ran out of the bay, down the corridor, and clanged up the stairs. She stopped and looked around the living room. Empty, except for slumbering furballs. Brie and Jeff were off gallivanting around the countryside, terrorizing any place with fresh produce. Kind of a Saturday morning ritual that didn't stop when the farmers' markets closed for the season.

The shower was on.

"How could she be taking a shower at a time like this?" Paula threw up her hands. "She'll need caffeine and food. I can do that."

She boiled water in the tea kettle and put a pile of cheese Danishes on a plate.

Cutty emerged from the bathroom in her terry cloth robe, wet hair sticking up every which way just as Paula was stirring the milk and sugar into the tea.

Paula picked up the tea and the plate of Danishes and rushed to her. "You found something?"

Cutty nodded. "Come on."

Paula eagerly followed Cutty into her room and put the tea and food on the desk.

"Bless you," Cutty said as she sat down and brought up the three video streams side by side. She adjusted them to start at the same chronological time. "Watch these while I get dressed."

Paula, brimming with curiosity, sat at the desk and clicked "play." She watched the woman in the cave with growing fascination.

"My god," she whispered.

"That's what I said." Cutty walked up behind her and picked up a Danish as she watched over her shoulder.

"She looks . . . panicked that she didn't find the fragment," Paula said.

"Panicked because it might lead investigators to her or because it's a part of an ancient, priceless sword?"

Paula turned to Cutty as she ran the possibilities through her mind. "If she thought the sword could be traced, it kind of fits our theory that the experts know this sword."

"But if they know the sword, they would also know its owner, or else she'd feel safe from discovery," Cutty said.

Paula covered her face and shook her head. "This is making my brain hurt."

"But wait, there's more." Cutty smirked as she leaned in and brought up the photo of the member of The Black Warriors.

"They do look alike," Paula said.

"And she was about a hundred miles away the night of this video in the cave," Cutty said. "Which means Jen missed catching her by a couple of hours, going by the time stamp and when it was uploaded to the cloud."

Paula stared at Cutty in amazement. "Seriously?"

"Yep." Cutty sat on the edge of the desk. "She's in the group The Black Warriors."

Paula stared, stunned, at the photo. "Seriously." Then her brain kicked into action. "Okay. We have software than can compare faces to determine if they're the same person."

"Totally cool." Cutty grinned.

"We have all kinds of neat software." Paula stood up. "I never thought we'd actually have the opportunity to use it."

"OKAY, I THINK I've figured it out." Paula made a few clicks with her mouse and crossed her fingers. "Looks like something is happening."

"It's trying to match the faces." Cutty watched the slow scan up and down and side to side of both faces in fascination. "Just like on *CSI*."

Paula laughed. "Yeah. Except they find the bad guy by the end of the hour."

"What I'm afraid of is we're going to find the bad guy and have no way of proving she did it," Cutty said.

Paula sighed. "I'm afraid the more we find, the further away we'll be from solving it."

The computer stopped scanning the faces and paused. Then a window filled with text popped up.

"It always says 'match' or 'no match' on TV," Cutty said.

Paula peered at the print. "This is way better. The more data, the more on our side if we have to argue it in court." She enlarged the window and sent it to the printer.

Cutty pulled the sheet from the printer. "Lots of data comparison." She looked up. "It's a match."

Paula took the sheet and pinned it up on the corkboard next to the two photos. Then she went to the half-filled white board and picked up a blue marker. "What's her name?"

Cutty blinked at Paula and reduced the face comparison program. She Googled The Black Warriors, and went to their website. "Okay. Her name's Alastrina Ni Cearnaigh. Strine for short. Born in Dunshanglin, Ireland. She's the drummer. Thirty-one, black hair, green eyes, six-foot one, favorite color, black. Hobbies, martial arts, running ultra-marathons, and"—she turned to Paula—"collecting ancient weapons."

Paula bit her lip and wrote Strine at the top of the board, followed by, "collects ancient weapons."

"Maybe someone used one of her swords and returned it with the missing piece." Cutty rubbed her chin as ideas pushed around in her mind. "Of course, she'd just send that person back to find the missing part."

Paula started a new column with "reasons to be in the cave" followed by "sword borrowed, returned with piece missing."

"Okay," she said. "What else?"

"She committed the crime and came back to look for the piece."

Paula jotted that down. "Was she in the area at the time of the crime?"

Cutty snapped her fingers. "Good question." She clicked on Tour Dates on the The Black Warriors site. She scrolled up to that fine day in October. Portland, Oregon. Before that, Seattle. After that, San Francisco. Three west coast cities in four days. She just couldn't skip out and fly halfway across the country. Not with interviews and sound checks and everything that would be demanding her time.

"Well?" Paula stood, watching her.

Cutty sighed. "She was in Portland, then San Francisco."

"So she couldn't have done it. Which leaves . . ." Paula put a check mark next to "sword borrowed."

Something niggled on the edge of Cutty's brain. Something that wasn't quite adding up. She opened her laptop, powered it up, and clicked on the cave videos.

"What?" Paula went to stand behind her.

"If she didn't do it, that means she's never been in the cave before." Cutty cued the videos to the moment Strine entered the cavern and let them run. A few seconds in, she stopped them, backed them up to the beginning and played back in slow motion. She stopped when Strine flashed the light on the incision. "See anything unusual?"

Paula sat down on the other chair. "Show it one more time. Slow."

Cutty reshowed the bit and stopped at the same place.

"She knew exactly where the sword hit the wall." Paula sat back, her eyes reflecting her racing thoughts. "Even if she had committed the crime, she wouldn't have been able to walk into a completely dark cave, turn on the flashlight, and point it right at a specific spot on the wall."

"And even if the person who committed the crime had explained where she hit the wall, she wouldn't have been able to give the exact spot, because she wouldn't have known the exact spot."

Cutty sat back and ran both hands through her hair. "My brain hurts."

"Right now we don't think, we just write things down." Paula patted her knees and stood up. "Then we'll get Brie and Jeff to look at everything."

"So all our brains will hurt?"

Paula laughed. "That's the normal state around here."

Chapter 11

PAULA DECIDED IT was hard to apply logical thought to illogical situations. She pushed her cart, already heavy with cat food and kitty litter, to the Health/Beauty department of the local super mart. She had volunteered to do everyone's mundane shopping. She seemed to do her best thinking in alien retail landscapes. Something about being surrounded by stuff she never knew existed much less had any desire to buy, except for the tiny fraction she did buy.

She pulled a crumpled list from her pocket. Toothpaste. Shampoo. Conditioner. She picked the items off the shelves with practiced efficiency and paused in the wide aisle to make sure she got everything on the list. Satisfied, she pushed the cart to the checkout area. Tuesday morning was the perfect time to shop, and clerks were actually waiting for someone to check out.

She shoved the cart through the automatic doors. The cold air went through her on a wind that gusted off the mountains. At least rain wasn't on the gusts. She looked up at the restless low clouds . . . yet. The cart bumped and lurched across the parking lot as she hurried to the car and heat. She opened the trunk and lifted the large bags of cat food into it.

"Isn't it a cliché for archivists to be cat lovers?"

Paula jerked up and turned around. A man—dapper popped into her mind—leaned against a pickup with an air of casual interest. He had on a fitted coat and scarf, pressed slacks, black polished shoes, conservative striped tie peeking out, neatly trimmed goatee, forties-style hat. The scent of Starbucks hung in the humid air between them. He was as out of place in the parking lot of a small town discount super mart as a polar bear.

"Cats seem to love us, so we feed them out of gratitude," Paula said. How does this man know who she is and what she does?

"I suppose they're good at keeping secrets." The man smoothed down his coat.

"Actually, they're lousy at keeping secrets." Paula finished loading her bags into the trunk and pushed down the lid. "But no one can understand them."

The man gazed at her for a moment, then gave a ghost of a smile. "You're only expected to archive the files in your care, not to investigate them."

Paula cocked her head. "Have you seen my job description?"

"I suspect it's the same as your predecessor."

Paula quirked an eyebrow. "He wasn't very good at his job."

"I disagree." The man pushed off the car. "He did his job very well. He understood the importance of, let's say, leaving some things a mystery."

Paula pulled a mints tin from her pocket and looked him up and down. "I think he was good at accepting monetary incentives for keeping some things a mystery."

Was that a flicker of surprise? The man lowered his eyes as he plucked off his gloves. He reached into his breast pocket and pulled out a thin silver case. "You might want to consider other possible . . . incentives . . . for leaving a few mysteries in the world." He opened the case and pulled out a card. "Some things are best left to time." He held out the card.

Paula stepped forward and took it.

"We will continue our chat." The man put the case back into a pocket and pulled his gloves on. "I know you'll demonstrate the good sense of your predecessor. Good day to you." He bowed his head.

As he turned around, Paula flipped open the mints tin, put her finger on a black dot from a row of black dots in a tiny numbered egg carton, and lightly swiped the back of his coat. Her little black bug clung to the wool. Blended quite nicely with it, too. He strolled at a good pace to the street. *So he didn't want me to see his car.* She went to the driver's side door, opened it, and climbed in. "I bet it's not a Kia."

She pulled out her phone, brought up her tracking app, and typed in the number for the black dot. A map popped up with a blip close by and moving away from her. "Number seven, enjoy the adventure." She punched in Jeff's number. "Hey. Busy?"

"Never too busy for boss biz," Jeff said.

"Want to do some stealthy reconnaissance?"

Jeff gave an exaggerated sigh. "You need to get a car that doesn't stick out like Lady Gaga at an Amish wedding."

Paula shook her head. Jeff prided himself on coming up with a new comparison every time he disparaged her car. "Get into the truck and follow tracker number 23."

"Yes, ma'am." Jeff actually giggled with glee.

"Have fun and pack some food and an overnight bag. I have the feeling this is going to be a road trip."

"Road trip."

Paula laughed. She could almost see him doing a happy dance.

She disconnected and looked at the card the man had given her. Seamus O'Hara. She squinted at the words below the name. "Looks like Gaelic." *Ciomeàdal dar fuil gaiscìoch.* The address was in Arlington. Not a surprise. The Hibernian League. Sounded like a rugby club. The emblem looked like a coat of arms. A single sword between the ornate letters F and G on a red shield.

"Hmmm. Guess I'll be brushing up on my Irish." She brought up the business card app on her phone and snapped the front and back of the card.

She took a little scanner from her pocket and ran it over both sides of the card. "That explains the extra period. Wonder if Mr. O'Hara has a good sense of humor . . ." She pulled out of the parking lot and headed for the Interstate to put the card on a semi heading in any direction but where she was going.

CUTTY PULLED THE casserole from the oven. Jeff had prepared a baked macaroni and cheese and put it in the refrigerator the night before. He insisted that it took a day for the flavors to meld together. The aroma was beyond heavenly. She was ready to grab a fork and eat it right out of the glass dish.

"So, this guy's straight from the Dan Brown lexicon of dapper bad guys." She put the casserole on a warming pad on the table.

Paula looked up from laying plates and silverware in front of three chairs. "Over the top in his own fantasy about himself or that organization he belongs to."

"And he hinted that he had convinced Mr. Christiansen not to investigate any crimes involving a sword."

Brie popped open three bottles of beer. "I'd be more impressed if he had convinced Mr. Christiansen to investigate."

Paula snorted a laugh. "Even if he wasn't ever going to try to solve the crimes, Mr. O'Hara didn't know Christiansen had an aversion to work."

"Money?" Brie put the bottles on the table and sat down.

Paula sat across from her. "No. Because I don't believe Mr. O'Hara."

"What?" Cutty sat down at the end of the table.

Paula scooped macaroni and cheese onto her plate and gave the serving spoon to Cutty. "There was something about the encounter that felt . . . I don't know . . . weak. Like all show without anything behind it."

Cutty plopped macaroni and cheese onto her plate and handed the spoon to Brie. She savored a mouthful. "Wow. This is amazing."

"We scoured the countryside for as many artisan cheeses as we could find," Brie said.

"Well worth the effort." Cutty swallowed another mouthful and waved her fork at Paula. "You think this is another expert expecting us to back away just because they said so."

Paula looked up at her. "That was it. I got the feeling he's used to getting his way. The kind of arrogance from someone who lives up here somewhere"—she leveled her hand above her head—"and expects everyone down here to not disagree with him."

Her tablet on the table woke up, and Jeff appeared on the screen.

She pushed up the volume. "What's up?"

"Save me some of that mac and cheese. I can smell it from here."

"If that were true, I'd hire your nose out as a lucrative side hustle," Paula said.

"Gawd help us." Brie stretched her arms out and looked up at the ceiling. "He's nosy enough as it is."

Cutty snorted a laugh.

"No more mac and cheese for Brie," Jeff said.

Brie threw up her hands. "Now he's a poet."

Paula chuckled. "We'll save you some if you tell us something entertaining."

"I have enough entertaining tidbits for a meal and leftovers and a couple of beers."

A live video feed replaced Jeff's face. Cutty squinted at the screen. Dark night, wet brick street with puddles disturbed by a light drizzle. Reflected streetlights were blurred and distorted from all the water. A building of light-colored stone stood across the narrow street. A small portico with columns more Greek influenced than Roman extended around a double door with a rough finish of wood that looked both heavy and ancient. The door latch was a long, ornate bar—dark, probably painted black—over a matching hook with a long tail in the shape of what looked like Celtic knots. The infamous Hibernian League perhaps?

"Tell the tale, oh wondrous wanderer." Paula propped the tablet against a beer bottle, and Brie and Cutty moved their chairs and plates so they could see the screen.

"Well, this is The Hibernian League headquarters." Jeff moved the camera around to show the whole building. "Not that it says it anywhere on the outside. But right next to the door is a mail slot with a plaque of that coat of arms on the biz card you sent me. Now here's the interesting part. Our dapper Danny boy is parked right over there." He panned to about a half block down the street. "It's the unpretentious black Lamborghini with the modest vanity plates that says BLD HERO."

"That certainly would have stood out in the super mart parking lot," Paula muttered.

"It even stands out here, and that's saying a lot," Jeff said. "Anyway, instead of getting out of the car right away, he waited until several men entered the building. The Hibernian League seems to be gents only."

"They're having a meeting tonight?" Cutty asked.

"Well, judging from the chatter"—Jeff held up a neat little listening device—"this was a regularly scheduled meeting. They chatted about other things that we can sort out later from the recordings."

"Were all these people as dapper as Mr. O'Hara?" Paula asked.

"I also have video, so we can break out the popcorn—"

Brie snorted. "When did we ever need *that* as an excuse?"

"It's a rather strange mix of people." Jeff aimed the camera back at the front door of the building. "The only common factor was they all looked very, uh, Hibernian. You'll see what I mean when you see the videos."

"O'Hara was just hanging out in his car, watching them?" Paula pulled a slice of garlic bread from the loaf.

"Yeah, basically, until this one guy walked by."

Jeff replaced the video stream with a photograph of two men, obscured by the rain and darkness penetrating the streetlights, huddled in an intense-looking conversation. The other man was heavyset in a muscular, rather than overeating kind of way. He looked as ill-fitted for the suit he was wearing as it was for him, and had a ruddy British Isles look. Cutty wouldn't be surprised to hear a brogue from him.

"I hope you were a fly on the wall for that one," Paula said.

"Fly wings intact and ever vigilant." Cutty could almost see Jeff performing a snappy salute. "The gist of the conversation was dapper Dan was telling the big guy that someone called S was being cagey about something, it sounded like Gaelic, we'll have to listen closely on the recording. Anyway, dapper Dan seemed pretty agitated about it and told the big guy to be ready with the fires. Whatever that means. He also emphasized that this tidbit was just between them for the time being."

"So things aren't all cozy and warm in the Hibernian League," Paula said.

"They seem a particularly serious bunch," Jeff said.

"Are you in DC?"

"Alexandria," Jeff said.

Brie shook her head. "I know where you're eating tonight."

"And staying." Jeff grinned.

"Glad we have a rich benefactor," Paula said.

Jeff grinned, and Brie guffawed.

"Looks like they're coming out," Jeff said. "I'll send all the videos and recordings when I have a chance."

CUTTY STARED AT the words on the white board and finally shook her head. "Keeper blood hero."

She had Googled *dar data* and scrunched her nose at the huge computer screen on the table next to the white board. "It means 'of.'"

Paula stared at the screen. "What an interesting language."

She wrote "of" beneath *dar data* on the board.

"Keeper of blood hero." Cutty frowned. "What was that discussion about, the fires one?"

Paula scrolled through the videos, sampling until she found the right one.

They watched with rapt curiosity as O'Hara approached the heavyset man. They huddled in the rain as O'Hara muttered in urgent tones. When the video was finished, Paula grabbed an oversize pad of newsprint and put it on a work table.

"Okay. Start it again," she said.

Cutty played the video in spurts while Paula jotted down the conversation, using syllables for the Irish.

Paula ripped the pages off of the pad and put them side by side. Cutty went to the worktable and read through the scribbles.

She picked up a red marker and circled two groups of syllables. "These look like blood hero."

Paula put her finger on the S. "O'Hara says, 'S isn't communicating with me.' The other guy says, 'You know how she is.'" She circled a space between a couple of lines with her finger. "This is where O'Hara gets in closer and is really intense. He says, 'Blood hero isn't back.' The other guy's reaction is extreme surprise."

"Like super shocked surprise." Cutty went to the laptop and played that segment of the video and paused on the man's expression.

"He says, 'That's not possible.' Then O'Hara almost growls, 'It's possible.' Play the section."

Cutty released the pause button. They watched the urgent exchange.

Cutty paused again on the big man's expression. "That's fear in his eyes. Like scared to death fear."

Paula studied the newsprint pages. "He says, 'It was in flawless condition.' O'Hara replies, more like hisses, 'Then why isn't it back?'"

Cutty played the video to that point. They stared at O'Hara's tense face.

"They're both scared," Cutty said.

"O'Hara continues, 'S will be at the Capital One Center two nights from now. I'll find out what's going on with her then. Be ready with the fire. The others must think everything is fine.'"

Paula blinked up and turned to Cutty, who was watching her wide-eyed.

"Oh my god," they said at the same time.

Chapter 12

CUTTY TRIED TO relax as the train rocketed much faster than the unnerving clickity clack seemed to indicate was possible. The trip had started out fine. They had caught the Metro out in the country at the East Falls Church Station. She thought it was cool that the platform was in the meridian between the opposing sides of highway 66. The train sailed through the Virginia countryside for a few minutes and then plunged into a never-ending tunnel. What was worse, the almost empty car got fuller at each stop until people were crushed together in the aisle as they hung onto the poles and swayed and jerked to the unnerving rhythm.

She would have never believed that she'd not enjoy something as simple as riding a subway. It was an adventure, something new. It was also loud and suffocating and kind of scary. Geez. People did this every day. No wonder their stress had stress.

"We're the next stop." Paula hung onto the seat in front of them as they swayed around a curve.

"Did we really go under the Potomac?" Cutty squished into Paula as the car went around another curve.

Paula gave her an amused look. "Yep."

"I'm glad I didn't know when we did." Cutty looked up at the garbled voice over the intercom.

Paula stood. "Let's make our way to the door."

Cutty clung to Paula's coat as they winnowed their way through the people in the aisle close enough to a door to make an escape. The car slowed down fast and Cutty grabbed a pole and hung on with all her strength as her body rocketed forward with the stopping car.

The doors whizzed open, and Cutty didn't even have a chance to recover her equilibrium as she was swept out onto the platform by a knot of people, with just as many people jumping on board.

Paula pulled her to the wall out of the surging stream of bodies. "Okay, let's get our bearings."

Cutty nodded as she raised her eyes and took in the soaring concrete arc with the arched walls and ceiling covered with rows of rectangular cutouts creating an Escher-like optical effect.

"Wow."

Paula looked up and grinned. "Pretty cool, huh?"

"Yeah." Cutty felt the tension dribble out of her.

"Okay." Paula showed Cutty the map on her phone. "We're a few blocks from Capital One Arena. We could get on another train and get off there, but I thought you'd like to walk a bit and see the city."

"I appreciate not getting on another train," Cutty said.

Paula laughed. "It'll be less crowded going home."

Cutty sighed. That would help.

"The escalators are this way." Paula winnowed around the crowd with Cutty so close she struggled not to step on the back of Paula's shoes.

They hopped on an escalator. Cutty stared up at the longest set of moving steps she'd ever seen. "We're pretty deep, huh?"

Paula flashed her an enigmatic look. "Keep to the right."

"What?" Cutty stepped to the right, as a woman in a business suit jogged by her. "Oh."

They finally reached the top of the escalator and headed to the bank of turnstiles.

Cutty stopped and frowned at the turnstile.

"Use your fare card." Paula held up hers and slipped it into the slot.

"Ah." Cutty pulled her card out of her jacket pocket and slipped it into the slot and caught it as she walked through.

She then looked up at an escalator even longer than the last one in a dramatic arched concrete tunnel. Natural light splashed the top steps.

"Whoa."

"You think the train ride was long." Paula skipped to the escalator and stepped on. Cutty scrambled after her and jumped on a moving step. "The longest escalator in the western hemisphere is in the Wheaton Station. It takes three minutes. This one only takes two minutes."

Several people rushed past them up the steps.

"Unless you're training for the hundred-meter escalator dash." Cutty grinned when the sprinters were stopped by a group of obvious tourists. "Maybe they should include hurdles."

"Most of them are already proficient in that as government workers." Paula nodded her chin at the relatively patient locals stuck behind the tourists. "If it was a weekday, and they were heading down, heaven help whoever was in their way."

Cutty grinned as the daylight seemed to flower around the top of the steps. As they approached the top, she was surprised to see the roof disappear, and the escalator deposited them right in front of the corner sidewalk. The cool air felt great after the stuffiness of the train.

Paula pulled her to the side into a small plaza of white stone.

Cutty couldn't help staring at the block-size buildings all around her. She looked up and down the street. The buildings seemed to go on forever in endless straight lines.

"Okay, the Capital One Center is that way." Paula pointed to the left. "It's the building blocking the road."

"How rude."

Paula turned the other way. "If you go about four blocks that way you're at the White House."

Cutty stared down the street of huge buildings. "Seriously?"

"Yep." Paula grinned. "But we're going the opposite way."

"I expect a grand tour of Washington at some point," Cutty said.

"Of course. Washington's a fun place to roam around in."

Cutty walk-ran after Paula, who seemed to automatically click into big-city pace as she skirted around an interesting mix of tourists, obvious Black Warrior fans, and Chinese. Cutty had done enough research to know they were in or near Chinatown.

"Excuse me," she muttered as a mantra as she tried not to collide with person after person.

Paula got to the corner and looked back. Cutty politely squeezed around a family speaking Italian, also waiting for the light.

"Sorry," Paula said. "Survival instinct kicks in when I'm in a city."

A bus roared up, squeaked to a stop next to them, and emitted a noisy cloud of stinky pollution.

"Nice." Cutty waved away the fumes.

"You learn to shallow breath," Paula said.

"So all the hyperventilation from living in the city isn't completely from stress."

"Don't say anything like that around here, someone will try to get a government grant to study it."

The bus pulled away, and Cutty looked across the street. A church and matching out buildings cut into a quarter of the block of new buildings. The church looked old, in a new-old kind of way. Like a new building based on old architectural style using old materials, making it even more of a curiosity because it hadn't been replaced by a more modern building.

"That's St. Patrick's Church." Paula stepped into the crosswalk as the light changed and walked at Cutty's pace. "It was the first parish established here and the first church building was on that spot. I think that's the third incarnation. It was finished in 1894 and the other buildings in the early twentieth century."

Cutty stopped walking and crossed her arms.

Paula stopped a step ahead of Cutty and turned around. "What?"

"How'd you become such a walking encyclopedia?"

"I tend to pick up stuff to read. It's a nervous tick." Paula shrugged, sheepishly.

"Well, you can always fall back being a tour guide if the bosses ever find out you're doing too much work and give you your walking papers."

They crossed the street, and Cutty got a better look at the church buildings. They were actually kind of quaint, made of brown stones with ocher mortar and paint around the windows and doors. Blue banners extended out over the sidewalk proclaiming Catholic Charities. Ancient-looking dark wood doors . . .

"Looks like the Hibernian League's door," she said.

Paula squinted across the street and turned back to keep walking. "Must be an Irish thing."

One of the doors opened, and Cutty grabbed Paula. "O'Hara just walked out of the Charities."

Paula gazed across the street. O'Hara was strolling toward the Capital One Center. "Glad I decided to wear my disguise all day. Come on."

Cutty stretched her legs to keep up with Paula and smiled at her idea of a disguise. All Paula had to do was slick down her short black hair and spike it into a fauxhawk. She had on tinted wire-rimmed glasses, a black Black Warriors T-shirt beneath a black leather jacket and blue jeans and boots. Silver chains hung from her silver studded belt. She even had white earbuds hanging out of the jacket pocket. Cutty had opted for the more casual fan look with a Black Warriors T-shirt under her jacket and jeans.

They crossed the street to the largest building Cutty had ever seen in person that wasn't a sports arena. From the catty-corner angle, it looked like a city block of white granite with Capitol Building façades on the two sides she could see. Greek style columns soared to porticoes with multi-story banners proclaiming new exhibits in vivid graphics between the columns.

"The Portrait Gallery," Paula said, as she used her taller vantage point to keep an eye on O'Hara.

"Wow." Cutty stayed right on Paula's heels as they skirted a busload of tourists. She kept her eyes on Paula's back and looked up surprised to find they had arrived at the bottom of the shallow granite steps that led to an entrance to the Gallery. A crowd, ballooning over the steps, funneled through the openings in the wall that supported the columns.

Paula casually joined the crowd until she was right behind O'Hara. Cutty raised an eyebrow and saddled up next to her.

They stared at O'Hara's black overcoat as they slowly climbed the steps.

Paula pulled out her phone and brought up an app that Cutty recognized as one of the "house" apps. She then slipped a mint tin from her pocket, flipped it open, and revealed several small black beads held in a tiny numbered egg carton. She punched a corresponding number on her app and it went from red to green. She picked up the bead next to the number and carefully attached it to the collar of O'Hara's coat.

They got to the top of the steps and squeezed into the space between the outer wall and the inner wall and a single revolving door. Paula followed O'Hara through the revolving door, Cutty pushed into a noisy white marble foyer with a pale wood information desk in front of her. Paula worked her way around the milling tourists, picked up a couple of gallery maps and brochures off the information desk, and handed one each to Cutty.

O'Hara walked around the desk to a pair of gold-framed glass doors. He pulled a door open and walked through.

"Act casual," Paula muttered as they went to the door.

She opened it and held it for Cutty to enter an airy courtyard—a relief from the warm, crowded foyer. The aroma of fresh healthy-type food tickled her nostrils as she took in the cool gray flagstone floor and white granite walls. Overhead was an amazing web of glass and beams, letting sunlight fill the area with a kind of calming peace, even with one section filled with people dining at tables and clumps of people all around the courtyard.

Paula studied the map and strolled to one of the long granite planters filled with flowers. Cutty walked next to her, pretending to check her phone for text messages. O'Hara walked with purpose to a tall, young woman dressed in black and wearing a black baseball cap. She wore wire-rimmed glasses and kept her head down. Of course, she didn't want to be recognized because the Gallery was full of Black Warrior fans hanging out before the concert. The Gallery was a free, not to mention warm, place to hang out in.

Paula sat down on the ledge-seat of the flower bed about ten feet from where the young woman stood. Cutty sat between her and several senior citizens resting their feet.

Cutty pushed a button on her phone and the scene in front of them appeared on the screen. Thanks to the feed from the camera in her beanie, she could zoom in closer on Strine.

O'Hara walked up to Strine. She was several inches taller than him, and he was average height.

"Start talking," he said.

Cutty jumped at his voice in her Bluetooth receiver. The directional microphone next to her camera really worked. Paula, also listening in with her own Bluetooth, gave her a thumbs up.

Strine shook her head and stared at the floor.

"Tell me what happened." O'Hara's voice was surprisingly gentle, almost fatherly.

"I'll take care of it." Strine didn't sound as if she thought she could take care of anything. Her musical lilt enhanced her melancholy expression.

"Just tell me." O'Hara put a hand on Strine's arm. She looked up at him. "It's an odd business we're in. Things can happen."

Strine sighed and stared at the ceiling. Cutty zoomed in on her face.

"I did the deed." The anguish and pain in Strine's striking green eyes was heartbreaking. "I was too late. He had started the countdown. I severed the main line of power hanging high on the wall to stop it." She bit her lip.

"What happened?"

"It got stuck in the wall." Strine sounded as miserable as she looked. "I pulled it free, and it disappeared from my hands. Then I . . . left."

"Why didn't you tell me there was a problem?" O'Hara's voice was still steady and soothing.

"I didn't know until you told me it hadn't returned. Only one reason for that, so I went back when we were close by." Strine raised her eyes to the glass ceiling. "I didn't find anything."

O'Hara nodded as if thinking over her words. "It's my job to get it back. *Ciomeádal dar datum fuil.* You shouldn't have kept what happened from me or tried to solve the problem yourself."

Strine straightened and gazed at him with what Cutty would call very compelling eyes. "My responsibility. No one has ever failed to return it. No one. I'm the first failure ever. It's my responsibility to restore my honor."

O'Hara's shoulders dropped. So maybe Paula was right. He was more bark than bite. He didn't really have the power he pretended to have.

He bowed his head. "At least, allow me to assist in your quest."

Strine gave him an enigmatic look that Cutty would call wary. "I need to know if anything has been written about this . . . situation. If there are ways to get it back. To track . . . just anything written about it." She glanced at the diver's watch on her wrist. "I have to get back." She took a step away from the wall and pinned O'Hara with a serious "don't mess with me" look. "Research only. I failed. I have to fix it." She held his eyes until he gave her a quick nod.

Strine put her head down and walked with long determined strides to the glass door. O'Hara watched her go through the doors and took out his phone.

"Goody. Bonus coverage," Paula mumbled.

"It's as I thought," O'Hara said into the phone.

He cast his eyes around the courtyard. Paula bent over as she studied the map, and Cutty pretended to be reading something on her phone. He glossed over them, along with everyone else. Disguise a success.

"Don't worry about anything except having the fires ready," O'Hara said. "It will appear when the piece is fired on the forge."

Cutty and Paula gave each other a surprised glance. Something concrete at last.

O'Hara pocketed his phone and strolled out of the courtyard.

Paula let out a long breath. "I guess we'd better batten down the hatches. I think we have something he wants."

"OKAY." PAULA RUBBED the sleep from her eyes as she sat in her favorite overstuffed chair.

Cutty, Brie, and Jeff were sprawled on the other furniture, munching their breakfast. Various cats were curled up in the free spaces like random furry punctuation marks.

"We have to think this through." Paula took a sip of coffee.

"Well, we can't let O'Hara get the fragment," Jeff said.

Paula bit her lip as something niggled on the edge of her mind. "First, let's dismiss the rather compelling elephant in the room."

Cutty, Brie, and Jeff blinked at one another.

"You mean the long shiny silver elephant?" Cutty asked.

"The very same," Paula said.

"Okay." Cutty nodded. "First off, the conversation was a study in vague references."

"What does it sound like they said?" Paula asked.

"I'll tell you what it sounded like to me." Brie put her fork on her plate and sat up. "Strine said she was too late, he had already started the countdown. Which means she killed him and realized he had set into place what she was trying to stop. The only way she could think to stop it was to cut the main power supply. She cut the cord, her sword got stuck, she pulled it out . . .''

Paula raised an eyebrow. "Yes?"

Brie sighed, picked up her fork, and gathered some egg onto it. "That's an awfully big elephant."

"Okay. Let's play count the pachyderms," Paula said.

"Well, I'd say the first one is how Strine knew about Mr. Jones and where he was and what he was up to," Cutty said.

"The trunked wonder is, how did she get in and out of the cave without leaving a trace?" Jeff said.

Cutty held up her empty fork. "Okay. The third tusked critter is a three-parter. How did the sword disappear, why didn't it reappear where it was supposed to, and why is the blade fragment still visible?"

Paula nibbled a maple-iced donut. "Let's start with the sword. Let's suspend physics and logic and personal beliefs about what's possible on *Star Trek*"—she gave Jeff a pointed look—"and take everything at face value. The sword arrives on the scene with Strine. From the way it sounds, the sword is kept in a special place"—she blinked up—"with O'Hara. He's the keeper."

Cutty cocked her head. "The keeper of blood hero. Blood hero's the sword?"

"Or he's Strine's keeper," Brie said. "Makes more sense that she's the blood hero."

"Except . . . he didn't act as if he had much control over her," Cutty said. "Face value? He's the keeper of the sword. She's the sword-wielder."

Paula nodded, trying to put a mental finger on that niggling thing.

"So why didn't the fragment disappear?" Jeff asked.

"Let's go through what we know," Paula said. "The sword appears with Strine. She kills Mr. Jones with it and, at this point, I would guess her mission would be done, and she'd go back to wherever she had been and the sword goes back to where it's kept. But that didn't happen. Somehow, whatever controls the swordbearer and the sword knew that the mission was not complete. Maybe the fact that she was still there alerted her to the fact that she had been too late."

"So she knows it's tied in with the electronics and cuts the power cord." Jeff swipes his fork like a sword. "The blade gets caught in the wall, and she pulls it free."

Cutty rubbed her chin. "The sword disappears from her hands, and she goes back to wherever she came from. As far as she's concerned, her mission was a success. She didn't fail."

"Then O'Hara tells her the sword didn't return," Jeff said. "But they didn't know what that really meant. Until we sent a sword expert photos of the fragment and our tests on the metal, and who must have shared the info with O'Hara."

"It sounds like they have this thing, this tradition that's a couple thousand years old, and they've never had the sword not come back." Paula held up a finger as another thought came to her. "And O'Hara is supposed to know the ancient text but didn't seem to know if there was anything in these texts to cover this situation. Except, he did have an idea what had happened . . . he said on the phone it was what he thought."

"And Strine seems to have figured it out because she went looking for the fragment," Cutty said.

"Funny O'Hara didn't tell her that we have it," Paula said.

The others looked up at her.

"Wonder why," Brie said.

Cutty held up her fork and swallowed a mouthful of food. "This is actually starting to make some sense . . . at least from the human dynamic angle. What if O'Hara is just the keeper of the sword? I'd say, within the Hibernian League, it's the highest and, most likely, a hereditary position. Since nothing has gone wrong on these missions, the people in this position have probably enjoyed the power without having to do anything to merit that power."

"Hereditary power," Brie said. "Inherited sense of entitlement and the confidence and arrogance that goes with it."

"What happens when an entitled, confident, arrogant person who has always had everything go right has the one important thing in their life goes wrong?"

"We forgot that this person is supposed to have learned the ancient text, but centuries of everything going right also leads to complacency." Paula nodded at the ideas buzzing around. They were on the right track. "I'm sure the keeper has been treated almost like an honorary position, and no one really studies the texts anymore."

"So he doesn't want to tell the league the sword is missing," Jeff said. "He only told the big guy, because he thinks he needs a smith to bring the sword back. He wants to fix the problem himself so no one finds out about what happened."

"Damage control," Cutty said.

Paula sat up and put her empty plate on the coffee table. "O'Hara thinks all they need is the fragment and a forge fire to bring the sword back." A fluffy charcoal-gray and white cat jumped into her now empty lap. She scratched behind its ear. "That means we'd have our murder weapon."

Cutty, Brie, and Jeff looked up and stared at her with intent expressions.

"What are you saying?" Jeff asked, warily.

Paula blinked at him. What was she trying to say? "I think I'm saying we have to let him steal the fragment from us." She almost laughed at their widening eyes. "We can't solve the crime without the murder weapon. We can't get the murder weapon unless it's made to reappear. The only way to do that is to let O'Hara steal the fragment."

"How are we going to do that?" Brie asked.

"Well, I think he's desperate enough to try to break in here and get it," Paula said.

"But he must know he'll get caught," Brie said.

"It won't stop him from trying." Paula steepled her fingers together. "And we want him to succeed." She looked at them and shrugged. "Let's make it easy for him."

"Leave it out in the parking lot with a little 'take me' sign?" Jeff asked. "I think he'd be a tad suspicious."

"I don't think Mr. O'Hara has a very high opinion of me, since I'm just an archivist playing a sleuth," Paula said.

Jeff gave her a wry look. "Think it might be your choice of transportation?"

"Or your penchant for wearing orange and red . . . together?" Brie said. "Archivists are supposed to be the ones with good fashion sense, not like regular librarians."

"Says the woman wearing Lynx head slippers," Paula said.

Brie lifted her feet and wiggled them. "Hey, gotta support my team."

"I don't think he'll be the least bit surprised if I naively visit a swordsmith with the fragment," Paula said.

"And how will he know you're going to do this?" Jeff asked. "His tracker doesn't work anymore."

Paula and Cutty exchanged wry glances. "We found his car. He had parked right on G Street in front of the Catholic Charities. We put a tracker on it, so we just wait until he's close by to scope the place, and I'll leave with the fragment in an important-looking metal case. That ought to get his curiosity up enough to follow me."

"So he follows you, and we follow him," Jeff said.

"I have a feeling O'Hara's going straight to this infamous forge the moment the fragment is in his hands," Paula said.

Cutty moved a cat off her lap and stood up, plate in hand. "You do know we've entered the land of fantasy fiction."

Paula nodded. "Yep."

Cutty gave a slow nod. "Okay. Just so we're all clear on that."

Chapter 13

CUTTY LEANED AGAINST Brie's Jeep Wrangler and breathed in the briny sea air. She watched the gulls swoop and dip around the white-bottom boats docked right up to where the old brick Annapolis streets met the Chesapeake Bay. The obvious groups of tourists didn't mask the profound feeling of history of the place. She wouldn't have been surprised to see colonial sailors tromping up and down the aged red brick street that stretched up the hill from the water, lined with tightly packed buildings—each with its own color of brick and character. Seaport really did describe this town.

They were parked in front of the Chesapeake Trading Company, a nice vantage point of where the street split, and if Cutty walked toward the water, she had a great view of the tiered white dome of the Maryland State House up the side street, a view of the marina on the water, and the tall steepled church at the top of St. Francis Street she was on. She was surrounded by colonial history.

She looked up St. Francis Street and saw Brie coming toward her with her long-legged stride and holding something in each hand. Cutty walked back to the Jeep and waited. She thought it ironic that they were parked across the street from an ice cream place, yet Brie insisted on hiking up the hill to the Annapolis Ice Cream Company for what she called mind-blowing ice cream.

Brie skipped up to Cutty and held out a paper cup with two very different-looking scoops in it. "You'll love what I got you."

"I'm afraid to ask." Cutty pulled the spoon from a scoop that had a fruity red-black running through a doughy beige.

"They looked so good, I got the same thing," Brie said.

"Now I'm really afraid." Cutty grinned as she licked the spoon. "Oh, wow."

Brie sampled her own. "That's the blackberry cobbler. Oh, man. That's good."

"What's the other one?" Cutty ate a spoonful of a fruity gold in doughy beige with spots of cinnamon. "Apple pie ala mode. I don't know which one I like the best."

"Equal opportunity love." Brie did a little happy shimmer as she dug into her ice cream.

Cutty laughed and worked on her own cup. The day was cool but not cold, the sun adding at least the impression of warmth. She caught sight of an orange vehicle going around the traffic circle in front of the harbor. "Erector set on wheels alert."

Brie looked up. "She'd better not hide it."

Cutty caught Brie's serious undertone. "You mean . . . ?"

"We traded cars in DC once. She hid it across the street from the Watergate. We had to figure out a series of clues to find it. I learned more about Foggy Bottom than I ever cared to."

Cutty snorted a laugh. "She must have found a spot close by." She nodded at Paula, who rounded the corner and strolled up the street toward them. She carried a slim metal briefcase. She walked between storefronts to a door with a swordsmith logo on it, opened it, and went inside.

O'Hara came out from around the corner across the street near the roundabout in front of the water. He trotted across the street to the door. He paused, as if listening through it, opened it, and walked in.

"You got the ice cream, I get to take the walk this time," Cutty said.

Brie waved her spoon. "Knock yourself out."

Cutty strode to the corner, finished up her ice cream, and dropped the cup into a trash can. She crossed the brick street and went down to where O'Hara had come from. It was a block-long one-way street with part of it open to a view of the water with cars parked nose to the curb.

"How convenient," she muttered as she spotted the black Lamborghini. She crossed the street and cut between the Lamborghini and an SUV that masked her from Francis Street.

She frowned at the sports car's angular frame. No convenient chrome fender to slip a tracker under. She had played lookout when Paula put the tracker on it in DC, so she didn't see where she had placed it. The tracker was black, so she attached it in the deep well that housed the headlight. She took out her phone and snapped photos through the heavily tinted windows. Probably a waste of memory, but there was always an off chance they could make out something interesting inside the car.

She went back to the front of the car and stepped onto the wide brick plaza with a few trees and bushes that separated the street from the roundabout. She walked back up to the Francis Street crosswalk, where the new asphalt met the old brick, and recrossed the street. She paused in front of a double storefront plus a single storefront down from the door

Paula had entered. The store on the corner was called Hats in the Belfry. Good enough for some extensive window shopping.

"Hope she's not much longer," she muttered. "Hats aren't really my thing."

She studied a rather rakish fedora on a rack of men's hats. She looked up the street and saw that Brie and the Jeep were gone. Main Street was one way up the hill, so Brie had to go around the block to get closer to the door.

The mid-morning sun ducked behind a random fluffy cloud, casting a chill over Cutty. She was always amazed how the world could change in a blink when the sun hid behind a cloud. In the window, she saw the reflection of a blue Jeep pull into a parking spot across from O'Hara's car on the short side street.

Brie was ready. She was ready. Now, all they could do was wait.

Her phone vibrated. She pulled it out of her pocket and smiled at the display. "Hey, Brie."

"Hey. I decided to give you something to do so you don't get arrested for loitering," Brie said.

"Or accused of spying for a rival hat company," Cutty said.

"Actually, that would probably come first." Brie laughed. "I suggest you walk slowly up to the next storefront as you talk."

"Where do you think O'Hara will go next?" Cutty asked as she started a cell phone meander.

"The forge could be anywhere," Brie said. "I just hope it's easy to follow him to it. These kinds of organizations tend to keep their important stuff in underground labyrinths guarded by nasty creatures from myth and fantasy."

Cutty grinned. "Yeah. I don't think there's an app for that."

"Heads up."

Cutty turned her head to the door maybe fifteen feet away from her.

O'Hara emerged from the doorway, metal case in hand, and walked straight across the street, barely checking for cars as he went. Cutty put her phone in her pocket and strode to the door before it closed and slipped inside.

She focused on the steep staircase that filled the dimly lit space to the second-floor swordsmith shop. Paula was sitting on a step about halfway up with her hands over her eyes. Cutty ran up the steps and knelt in front of her.

"What happened?"

"Maced." Paula raised her head, eyes closed, tears seeping out beneath the lids. "Stings like crazy, but he didn't take the time to give me a good dose. Just enough to grab the case and run. My glasses stopped a direct hit."

"Let's get you to the car." Cutty helped her up and they leaned, shuffled, and stepped down the stairs, then stopped at the door.

Cutty squinted through the textured glass. Her phone buzzed. "Yes."

"He's getting into the car," Brie said.

"Now I know what the milk and towel are for." Cutty gave Paula a wry look.

"Peppered?"

"Yep."

"Ouch." Cutty could hear Brie's wince. "Okay, he's pulling out . . . turning on Main . . . Okay. Coast is clear. See ya in a sec."

Cutty heard the Jeep start up then the phone disconnected.

"Lower your eyes so the sun doesn't kill you." She shoved the door open and helped Paula step outside.

Paula covered her eyes and turned away from the sun. "That officially doesn't feel great."

Brie double parked in front of them and jumped out of the still running Jeep. Cutty handed Paula to her so she could get her into the passenger side. Cutty hopped into the driver's seat and helped Paula settle in and get her seat belt buckled.

"Got the key to the thing?" she asked Brie.

Brie patted her pocket. "Right here. Take care of my baby."

"I'll treat her like she's my own."

"In loving hands." Brie grinned as she shut the passenger door.

Cutty grabbed the carton of milk, a towel, and a box of tissues from the back seat and piled them on Paula's lap.

"Thanks," Paula said.

"Too bad the only thing for the sting is your own tears." Cutty put on her seat belt and checked the GPS display on the dash. Brie had programmed O'Hara's tracker.

She put the Jeep into gear and eased into the light traffic. She drove up the hill and turned onto Church Street, which circled one way to the north around the old red brick church with the spire.

She looked back at the intersection they had just driven through. "Okay. Didn't turn to get to 70 and the highway." She looked at the GPS. "He took West Street."

She turned onto a street that looked nearly as ancient as the streets near the water. A Tudor-style building stood on the corner and the road had an old, rustic feel to it.

"Glad we filled the tank before we got here."

Paula blinked at her.

"He's headed more south than west."

"Might be a short cut or another stop." Paula poured milk onto the towel and held it to her eyes.

"Getting a scenic ride through town." Cutty drove past the very impressive white stone buildings of the Westin Hotel. "Okay. Another roundabout." She turned north into the one-way traffic. "He didn't turn on the road to 70. He turned south on Spa Road."

Paula frowned as she squinted at the GPS. "It's still too blurry."

The buildings were getting sparse and the trees along the road grew denser and less cultivated with pockets of older-looking subdivisions. She jogged off on Hilltop Lane and came to a streetlight. "I'm turning west on 665."

"We're south of the highway but paralleling it," Paula said.

"Back to civilization." Cutty looked around at the buildings and neighborhoods. "Are we still in Annapolis?"

"Yeah." Paula shaded her eyes and blinked out the window. "It sprawls all over the peninsula." She frowned as she studied the GPS display. "665 runs into 70, but why would he take such an out of the way route to get there?"

"We're getting off up here." Cutty took the off ramp to a stoplight. A huge shopping center was across the road. A replica of the Cape Hatteras Lighthouse rose from a mess of buildings. "We're turning south instead of north."

"South." Paula pressed the towel to her eyes again. "Interesting."

Cutty gave her a sidelong look as she turned onto the multi-lane highway. "We're on highway 2."

Ahead, the trees and urban sprawl disappeared into the countryside with the occasional farmhouse and gently rolling farmland. Just as quickly, the trees thinned, and they were passing a low white building with boats lined up around it and the road arched upward ahead.

"Is that a bridge?"

"We have to get off the peninsula somehow," Paula said.

Cutty drove onto the bridge. Marinas filled with boats sprawled on either side. The land on the ragged edges of water was covered with trees.

Marinas clustered around the southern shore as she sped back onto dry land.

"Looks like we're in for an interesting drive," Paula said.

"Now I'm really glad we filled the tank," Cutty muttered.

THREE HOURS OF scenic foresty, swampy, watery back roads of Maryland and Virginia in a bumpy Jeep while holding a milky towel to her stinging eyes and skin . . . Not one of Paula's more enjoyable experiences.

Cutty rolled off the last of a dozen two lanes with varying degrees of quality surface material onto highway 64 going south—an old highway surrounded by thick forests. The lanes going north were almost hidden by trees and dense vegetation in the thick medium between the lanes. The smoother road felt like heaven.

"Okay. Williamsburg or Jamestown?" Paula asked.

Cutty glanced at her. "Not Yorktown?"

"I don't recall a blacksmith there." Paula stared at the tangle of vegetation flowing by.

"Maybe the big guy's a re-enactor and he has his own forge," Cutty said.

"Down here that's possible." Paula looked at the GPS. "He's turning off on 143. Williamsburg."

Cutty grinned. "I've always wanted to see Williamsburg."

"You have to spend a few days to see it all," Paula said. "Lots of history happened down here."

"I've always been fascinated by Jamestown." Cutty took the 143 off ramp They had caught up with O'Hara in one of the tiny towns when he had pulled into a convenience store for a few minutes. The challenge since then had been keeping far enough back to be out of sight on the almost deserted back roads.

They merged onto a scenic parkway.

"Jamestown Island is the spookiest place I've ever visited." Paula shivered at the thought of it.

"Seriously?" Cutty followed O'Hara's meanderings into town.

"Oh, yeah. Ride around it at dusk sometime. Spooooky." The blip on the GPS stopped. Paula studied the display. "Looks like he's on the edge of the Colonial part."

"What do I do?" Cutty turned onto Francis Street, and they were surrounded by white colonial houses and buildings. She gazed out the window. "Cool."

"He parked in the lot up ahead." Paula pointed. "Right after that crosswalk. To the left. Go into it and park in the far-left section."

Cutty turned and bumped over an orange cobblestone sidewalk into a dusty lane that opened into a large, segmented parking lot. She turned left at the first segment and found a spot at the farthest end from the entrance. Near a quaint white house with a white picket fence.

Paula put on a baseball cap and exchanged her white jacket for her black leather jacket. Enough of a change not to bring attention to herself.

"How are we going to follow him?" Cutty asked as they slipped out of the Jeep.

"I put a tracker on the fragment," Paula said.

"What if he saw it?" Cutty stretched out her back as Paula joined her.

"I gambled that he was so anxious to get here, he wouldn't even take it out of the plastic bag." Paula slipped on her prescription sunglasses. Her eyes still watered and her skin felt on fire. She then pulled her phone out and brought up her tracker app.

Cutty nodded at the display. "I think your gamble paid off."

"Yep." Paula spotted what looked like a shortcut to Francis Street. "Time to run."

They trotted to an adjacent parking area bordered by dormant gardens and a couple of white wood-framed houses. They went through a gate of the ubiquitous white picket fence that opened up on Francis Street.

"Have your badge ready to flash," Paula said.

They dodged around a group of tourists chattering in Japanese and ran through a dirt entrance in the picket fence across the street.

"The long white building." Paula ran up to a man in colonial dress near the entrance of the building. Fortunately, only a few tourists were around. Thank god it was mid-week in November.

She held up an FBI badge she had borrowed from an evidence box that included an impressive collection of counterfeit items, and Cutty held up her police chief badge.

Paula bent her head to the man and said in a low voice, "We don't want to alarm anyone. We're just investigating a report related to an ongoing case. Could you hold people from entering while we look around and make sure everything is safe?"

The be-speckled man blinked at her in surprise.

"Thanks." Paula and Cutty rushed past him and through the door of the long white building. She hoped the man gave them the benefit of the doubt and did as she asked.

Paula blinked around the long interior. She counted four forges with their own red brick fireplaces and a wall housing the bellows in front of them. O'Hara was standing near a forge in the corner, next to the back exit. Several tourists were at that forge, watching a demonstration. The blacksmith was the man O'Hara had talked to outside the Hibernian League, and he kept darting anxious looks at O'Hara as he continued to entertain his audience.

She exchanged a look with Cutty. Cutty strolled around, gazing at the different items on display and putting herself in front of the blacksmith closest to O'Hara.

Paula went to another forge and angled herself so she could watch O'Hara.

The blacksmith's assistant at her forge worked the noisy bellows and the rise of heat spreading over the glowing coals burned her sensitive skin. She squinted to squeeze the tears from her eyes to stop the stinging. Maybe she could get some ice cream and apply it directly to her face. Her blacksmith hammered the glowing thing in his tongs and plunged it hissing into a bucket of water. The odd aroma of vaporized water and metal rose up around Paula. He held up the ornamental piece to the appreciative murmurs of his small audience.

Demonstration over, most of the people went out of the building through the exit door near O'Hara's forge. Paula went to the fireplace and studied the bellows. The hammering at O'Hara's forge stopped, followed by a splash and hiss. She half turned, pretending to study an ornament on display and saw O'Hara glance around the room. The blacksmith poured some liquid on the anvil. A magic elixir?

O'Hara put something—had to be the fragment—on the anvil. The blacksmith stared at it for a few seconds with an expression of uncertainty and possibly fear. He picked up the fragment with his tongs and plunged it into the glowing coals. After a few minutes it glowed orange. He pulled it out, held it on the anvil, and picked up a hammer. He gave O'Hara a look of even greater fear and uncertainty.

"Do it," O'Hara said through his teeth.

The blacksmith lifted the hammer and hit the fragment. He stared at it and blinked up at O'Hara. His eyes were almost accusatory.

"Again," O'Hara growled.

"Risk hurting it?" The blacksmith's voice was strained with fear.

"Again." O'Hara's body stiffened. Anger? Uncertainty?

The blacksmith hit the fragment. He stared at it. Nothing.

O'Hara bent over it. "Impossible. The ancient texts—"

"Are wrong." The blacksmith plunged the fragment into the bucket of water and left it in there.

Paula caught Cutty's eye and signaled for her to go out the back exit. Cutty nodded and walked out of the building.

"I'll be back with the right way to do it." O'Hara grabbed the tongs and fished the fragment out of the bucket. He wrapped it in a soft cloth and slipped it into his pocket.

He gave the blacksmith a withering look and strode to the exit.

Paula waited a few seconds, put her hands in her pockets, and strolled past the blacksmith, who seemed lost in his own stricken thoughts, and paused in the opened exit door. She crossed her arms and let a smile dance around her lips. O'Hara was bent over with his hands covering his eyes and making some rather undignified sounds of agony. Cutty was tucking the soft cloth into her pocket. Paula put a finger to her lips. She didn't want O'Hara to hear them, especially her. She signaled with her head, and they followed the path around to the front of the building.

Paula walked up to Colonial actor, who was dutifully holding back a small line of tourists. "Thank you so much. Fortunately, it was a false alarm. Have a nice day." She hurried away before he had a chance to say anything.

Cutty sidled up to Paula. "What now?"

Paula glanced at her. "Dinner?"

"What about O'Hara?" Cutty asked.

"Put the tracker on him?"

"Yep."

"He won't be able to drive for a while, so we may as well take advantage of where we are for dinner."

"Is that where we're heading?"

They emerged onto the Duke of Gloucester Street.

Cutty gawked all around her. "Wow."

Paula grinned. Gloucester Street was a showcase of shops and taverns from Colonial times. She stopped them in the middle of the dirt road. "If you look that way, you see the original capital building. If you look that way"—they faced the other way—"you'll see the Christopher Wren building on the William and Mary College campus."

"Double wow." Cutty turned in a circle, taking in all the buildings. "I really need to come back here some time and explore."

"To begin your introduction"—Paula walked to a large white building with seven gables—"we'll dine at Chownings Tavern for the best Welsh rarebit you'll ever have."

Cutty grinned. "Sounds great."

Chapter 14

"BOY, THEY'RE NOT kidding when they do things the old ways." Cutty strolled up to the placard on the old Presbyterian Church. "Eating by candlelight, everyone in costume and in character, with all the thees and thous."

"All a part of the fun." Paula studied her tracker. "He's still at the blacksmith's." She looked down the crossroad they were passing. "I have an idea."

Cutty laughed. "I'm beginning to love your ideas."

She took advantage of the impromptu tour of Williamsburg and gawked at the houses and gardens as they passed by. She had never imagined it to be so . . . authentic. But, then it was an archeology dig first and authentic meticulous reconstruction of the original buildings second. The sky grayed and the streetlights were sparse, and she could imagine what it must have been like to live there all those centuries ago.

She realized they were in a parking lot and that black car looked an awful lot like . . . "What are you up to?"

"Just taking out some insurance for the night." Paula walked to the front of the Lamborghini.

"You know that has an alarm system on it." Cutty crossed her arms and watched Paula with amusement.

"Last I heard, they don't cover tires."

"You're going to puncture his tires?"

"Well, I don't have any toilet paper to t.p. it with." Paula shrugged. "Of course, if we had spray paint . . . that would be fun."

Cutty snorted a laugh. "So I guess we're stuck with mundane vandalism."

Paula fished out of her jacket pocket her super cool custom-made imitation of the biggest, baddest Swiss Army knife. The thing was a good five inches thick with dozens of tools compactly folded into it. She pulled open a tool that looked like a tire gauge.

"Wanna bet they're steel-belted?" Cutty asked.

"That's why I'm doing this." Paula knelt beside the front passenger tire and twisted off the air cap. She pushed the tire gauge into the valve stem and twisted it. Cutty could hear the hiss of air escaping. Paula looked up. "One down, three to go."

"You're bad," Cutty said in admiration.

Paula chuckled gleefully as she ran around to each tire and let the air out.

"Now what?" Cutty asked.

"We check into the B&B Jeff booked for us, and then go to the King's Arms Tavern for their bread pudding and apple cider rum toddy and exchange war stories," Paula said.

Cutty cocked her head. "Ya know. I like the way you think."

PAULA TOOK A sip of the apple cider rum toddy and closed her eyes as the warmth trickled down her throat. She was glad she took a few minutes for a quick shower to remove the rest of the mace and the sticky milk.

Cutty sipped her toddy and moaned. "That's so good. And warming." She looked around the smallish room with doors to other small rooms. The walls were painted white as was the fireplace opposite them.

Their server, a cheerful woman in colonial dress was demonstrating how to use the huge white linen napkin on a hapless tourist as she explained its uses and traditions.

"I love the lamps." Paula nodded at the tall candlestick with an equally tall candle, inside a carafe-shaped glass with no top or bottom. "It's so simple and ingenious. Just a candlestick and an easily removable glass protector."

"And it's amazing how much light the candle gives off." Cutty grinned as their server put a white plate with a mound of bread pudding swimming in a fragrant bourbon custard sauce and topped with a sprig of peppermint and a strawberry slice in the middle of their small table.

"Mr. Jefferson's favorite bread pudding for the ladies," their server said. "Enjoy."

"Thank you, we will," Paula said.

Cutty picked up the dessert spoon. "Shall we take the first bite together?"

Paula smiled at the slightly romantic impulse. The candlelight did make it feel a bit like a date. An easy thought to have sitting across from Cutty. She picked up her spoon and poised it over the pudding.

Cutty laughed as they plunged their spoons in together and quickly swept the dripping spoonfuls to their mouths.

Paula savored the bourbony, custardy, cinnamony goodness. Just as she remembered it.

Her phone buzzed. Darn, she was enjoying just spending some down time with Cutty. She hadn't hung out with someone who was just fun to be with in a long time.

She pulled her phone from her pocket. Jeff.

Cutty sighed as she paused in digging out another spoonful of pudding.

Paula put the phone to her ear. "It better be good."

"He wants to talk to you," Jeff said.

Paula gazed longingly at the pudding. "And you know this how?"

"He called the swordsmith in Annapolis and told him to give the message to you. You had the good sense to give them the house number."

"So did he leave a way of contacting him?" Paula took a sip of the hot toddy and rolled her eyes at Cutty.

"Yep. I'll text it to you," Jeff said. "Do I have to remind you to use good sense?"

"Uh"—Paula focused on the deep brown wood table—"I'll make sure he doesn't get the fragment back."

"Yeah, that would kind of defeat the purpose of this whole adventure," Jeff said.

"Oh, I don't know"—Paula winked at Cutty—"Cutty's been enjoying her visit to beautiful Colonial Williamsburg."

"Yeah, and the cozy B&B isn't anything to sneeze at either," Jeff said.

Paula glanced at Cutty. Maybe even cozier on a more extended visit sometime. "Sorry the bread pudding doesn't travel well."

"Grrrr."

"Later, Jeff." Paula smiled as she disconnected.

Cutty raised an eyebrow.

"It seems O'Hara wants to have a chat." Paula sipped her toddy.

"I bet he does," Cutty said.

"Wanna bet he's staying in the Williamsburg Inn?"

Cutty frowned. "Not with the blacksmith?"

"He's parked in a lot near the Inn and can't move," Paula said. "And could you picture him staying anywhere else?"

"Putting it that way . . ." Cutty spooned out more bread pudding. "Wonder where his money comes from."

"He doesn't seem to have a regimented everyday job." Paula shrugged as she gathered more pudding onto her spoon.

"Old money maybe?" Cutty asked.

"Probably from the pot of ancient Celtic gold at the end of the rainbow where they keep the sword." Paula sighed and read Jeff's text. "He's not going anywhere, and we have this nice hot toddy and dessert to savor. Not to mention this cozy and relaxing atmosphere. Gotta take advantage of it when you can."

Cutty held up her hot toddy. "I like the way you think."

CUTTY FOLLOWED PAULA into the spacious colonial-style suite and plopped down onto one of the overstuffed chairs facing the fireplace. She looked like what Paula was feeling—too much hot toddy and rich dessert, not to mention a rich dinner on top of a long adventurous day.

Paula sat in the other chair facing the fireplace. "Let's see what he wants, other than the obvious."

"This ought to be interesting." Cutty settled back into the chair with her hands folded on her stomach.

Paula flourished her phone, punched the number from Jeff's text, and put it on speaker.

"O'Hara," a voice barked.

"Reisling." Paula propped the phone against a stack of old books on the coffee table in front of her and Cutty.

O'Hara sighed. "We need to stop playing games."

"Getting maced is playing a game?" Paula arched an eyebrow at Cutty, who gave her a comical face.

"Very unpleasant, I admit."

He didn't mention the car. He probably didn't notice the flat tires in the dark and with stinging eyes. The advantage of steel-belted tires. Also all but confirming he's staying in the Williamsburg Inn.

"I'll stop playing if you come clean about what's going on," Paula said.

O'Hara took in an impatient breath. "There are secrets that must remain in the world."

"I'm not a Dan Brown fan." Paula rolled her eyes at Cutty.

"I'm not going to beat around the bush," O'Hara said. "I have to have that blade, and you have to forget all about any of this."

Paula frowned. Are we at check already? The hot toddy hadn't even had time to kill off more brain cells. "I think . . . you're not the one I should be talking to about this."

She smiled at the stilled silence from O'Hara. "I'm the only person to talk to."

Paula chuckled. "That's obviously not true."

"Why do you say that?" O'Hara's voice was hard. Paula wondered how much it would take to make it brittle enough to break.

"I hear things." Paula pulled off her glasses and polished them with her shirt end. "I heard you weren't happy about what happened with the blacksmith."

"I got careless to let someone follow me," O'Hara said.

"I prefer the term amateurish." Paula smiled at Cutty's surprised expression.

O'Hara's silence was of the shocked variety. "You'd guard your words closer if you knew who you were talking to."

"I know I've been talking to the wrong person," Paula said. "That's all I need to know about you."

"Says the woman who carelessly let the blade be stolen." O'Hara's bravado returned.

"Says the man who carelessly let the blade be stolen back." Paula was having too much fun. The only thing that would make it more fun was if she could get him to lower his guard and spill something interesting. "So, what made you so angry at the forge?"

"I don't have to tell you anything," O'Hara said.

"What I don't understand is why you would go to all the trouble to steal something and then want to put it in a forge fire and hammer it." Paula paused. "Other than wanting to destroy evidence in a crime. But I can think of less dramatic ways to do that."

"There are mysteries . . ."

"Yeah, yeah." Paula waved her hand. "The only thing about that . . . you don't seem to have a solid grasp on those mysteries and secrets, from your anger at the forge."

"You don't know anything about it." O'Hara's brittle voice cracked.

"Enlighten me. I'm a good listener."

"Hah!" O'Hara's anger almost radiated through the phone. "You just got lucky. You're just a glorified librarian."

Paula laughed. "I'll send you my academic transcripts. You might find them entertaining and enlightening." She pulled her tablet from her mini-backpack, powered it on, and brought up her tracking app. Yep. Just as she thought.

"I've been trying to make this so it won't be embarrassing to you with your bosses," O'Hara said.

"How considerate," Paula said. "You're assuming they don't know what I'm doing."

She brought up her browser and searched "Pizza" and "Williamsburg, Virginia." Cutty looked at her as if she had lost her mind.

"They'll care when you stick your nose in too deep where it isn't supposed to go," O'Hara said.

"There's a class in archivist school called Sticking Your Nose in Too Deep 501," Paula said. "A very important class for learning how to do research."

Cutty covered her mouth to muffle her laugh.

O'Hara seemed to be taking steadying breaths. "All right, Ms. Reisling. I've tried to give you a chance to do the right thing and back away from this. I'm afraid the gloves are coming off. I will get the blade fragment back, and you will stop your investigation—one way or another."

"No, you won't," Paula said. "For one simple reason."

"And what is that?"

"You're just a lackey without a clue of what you're really doing." Paula smiled at his audio fuming.

"It'll be a pleasure to witness you eat your words," O'Hara said.

"You don't have the right kind of mustard to go with those words." Paula grinned as Cutty doubled over with silent laughter.

"Watch your back. I won't be as . . . humane . . . next time." O'Hara disconnected.

Paula put down the phone. "That was fun."

"Nothing like capping off a pleasant evening with a few empty threats." Cutty sat up and stretched.

"In every clichéd, B-movie way." Paula rubbed her chin as she contemplated the blinking green spot on her tracking app. "He thinks he's in charge of this situation. We just have to keep reminding him he's not, while we go after who we should really be talking to."

Cutty cocked her head. "You mean Strine?"

"Yep." Paula sat forward. "I think she knows something O'Hara doesn't. I just thought about it after today's display of ineptitude at the forge."

"Strine thinks she's the only one who can fix it," Cutty said.

Paula gazed at her. "Yes. If the deed—the magic—can only happen by her hand, then any way to fix the magic would be at her hand."

"So we need to get the fragment into her hands," Cutty said. "Without O'Hara knowing about it."

"It's interesting O'Hara didn't tell her the fragment has been found," Paula said.

Cutty spread out her hands. "He wants to be the hero in this. He wants to prove he has power he obviously doesn't have."

"Speaking of . . ." She picked up her phone and punched in Jeff's number. "Hey. Wanna have some fun?"

"Do you have to ask?" Jeff asked.

"I want you to find Jack's Pizza in Williamsburg," Paula said. "Order five of their largest, most expensive pizzas and some garlic bread, and, oh yeah, they have wings. So order their biggest order of wings. You're Seamus O'Hara at the Williamsburg Inn, and you'll be paying in cash."

Jeff chuckled. "You're so bad."

"Just letting him know we know where he is, even though he doesn't know where we are," Paula said.

"I'm on it, boss," Jeff said. "Enjoy the fancy room."

"You bet." Paula grinned. "These are perks I can get used to."

"And the company ain't bad either." Cutty lifted her bottle of water in a salute.

Paula, grinning with delight, picked up a bottle from the table and returned the salute. "I'll second that."

Chapter 15

CUTTY SPRAWLED ON her back on the living room sofa as she watched the video of Strine's and O'Hara's encounter in the Portrait Gallery on her tablet for the umpteenth time. She watched it without sound so she could concentrate on Strine's body language.

The aromas from the kitchen were driving her crazy. It was Greek night—and not in the frat house toga wearing sense either. Jeff had spent a good part of the afternoon cooking up a feast.

Paula was wandering in and out of the rooms lining the living room, making phone call after phone call. She was trying to track down Strine now that her concert tour was over.

The sound of a bouncing basketball and the jingle of a basket reverberated from the main floor. Brie was working on her three-point shot. She said it was never too late to get invited to the Minnesota Lynx training camp.

Cutty stopped the video on Strine's anguished face. Anguished and determined. Not the face of someone who was subservient or someone who answered to another person. The anguish in her eyes was the kind found in leaders with the full responsibility of the world on their shoulders.

Cutty sucked in her breath and gazed at the pipe hanging from the ceiling above her. "She really *is* in charge . . . of whatever is going on here."

She put in her ear buds, pushed play, and then stopped at the moment Strine said, "My responsibility." Strine not only looked like someone taking responsibility, she looked like someone who was the only one who had the responsibility. She turned up the volume and replayed the section. "It's my responsibility to restore my honor."

My honor, not *their* honor—the honor of the Hibernian League.

"Oh, thank you, thank you." Paula wandered out of Jeff's room, still on the phone. "I owe you big time. Thanks." She disconnected and grinned at Cutty. "Get packed, we're going to Trinidad."

Cutty sat up and returned the grin. Trinidad. Hot, sun, beaches . . .

"Don't forget to pack sweaters and something rainproof," Paula tossed over her shoulder as she walked into her room.

PAULA TRIED NOT to laugh as Cutty stopped at the bottom of the steps of a small plane and looked as if she wanted to kiss the ground. The turbulence had been less than pleasant for much of the ride from Los Angeles.

"Let's get inside." Paula took Cutty's arm and led her into the surprisingly airy Arcata-Eureka Airport and dragged her out of the stream of people traffic.

"God," Cutty muttered. "I don't have any nerves left."

Paula grinned. Her own nerves were jarred from the bumpy ride. "All these small planes are like that."

"Just when I was getting used to flying." Cutty straightened and settled her small backpack on her back. "The plane to Los Angeles, not to mention first class, lulled me into false expectations."

"Enjoy first class when you can, because most of the time travel won't be so cushy." Paula adjusted her backpack and looked around. "The baggage claim is over there."

She was pleased they blended in with the casual laid-back people around them, interspersed with the ubiquitous business type. They looked like a pair of outdoors enthusiasts ready to conquer the rugged coastal trails of Northern California. She had to admit Cutty came by the look naturally, being an avid hiker with the worn, lived-in wardrobe to match.

They stopped in front of the baggage carousel. Paula glanced around. She knew O'Hara hadn't figured out they knew about Strine, but he could be paranoid enough to have someone hanging around the airport. Trinidad was small enough that anyone who wasn't a native and didn't act like a tourist stood out.

Their hiking backpacks came around to them on the carousel, and they pulled them off.

Cutty took off her small backpack and tied it onto the larger one. "I kind of wish we were really going hiking."

"Well, at least you'll be able to get the lay of the land. In case you want to come back to explore in the future." Paula shouldered her pack and groaned a little from the weight. She marveled how hikers could walk through rugged wilderness carrying so much weight on their backs, while she could barely make it between airport gates.

They walked out through the sliding front doors into a misty, partially overcast day, cool enough for the fleece jackets they wore.

Cutty looked up and around. "It feels . . . I don't know . . . different."

"Pacific coastal." Paula breathed in the moist air, heavy with briny overtones. She looked around. The parking lot was across the street. "This way."

"Where's sunny California?" Cutty peered at the low, rather menacing clouds as she kept pace with Paula through the parking lot.

"In the way southern part of the state," Paula said. "This is the cool, rainy, foggy part of the state."

Cutty cocked her head and breathed in the air. "It's so peaceful and quiet. Still. I like it."

"Ah"—Paula held up a finger—"you're an ocean person."

"It is close by?" Cutty squinted into the mist.

"That lighter line of gray beyond that white-roofed building over there." Paula pointed ahead of them.

Cutty stood on her tiptoes and shaded her eyes. "That's the ocean?"

"Yep."

"Cool." Cutty grinned. "What are we looking for?" The sizable parking lot was about half full of cars.

Paula shrugged. "Chris said I'd know it when I saw it."

Cutty gave her an amazed look. "Really?"

Paula walked to the middle of the lot. "I spent the summer between my junior and senior year here. Chris spent two semesters telling me about this part of California, so I knew I had to see it for myself."

She stopped in front of a car and gazed at it with arms crossed.

Cutty stopped next to her and frowned at an ancient VW bug painted like a hippie psychedelic poster. "You're kidding."

"This is a major hippie haven," Paula said. "Pretty much stuck in the sixties in a lot of ways."

"You embraced your inner hippie when you were here?" Cutty asked.

Paula blinked at her in surprise. "Liberated was more like it. I bought this car the day after I arrived, and Chris and I painted it. She said she'd keep it, and it looks like she did."

"Looks like she kept it in good condition," Cutty said.

Paula walked around the car, nodding in appreciation. "I always said I was going to live here when I retired."

Cutty laughed. "I'd pay to see you tooling around in that car as a gray-haired old lady."

"That's not a unique sight around here." Paula went to the passenger side and popped open the gas tank door. She took out a key chain with a peace symbol and a couple of keys dangling from it.

"That's a strange place for the gas tank," Cutty said.

"It's in the front and the engine is in the back." Paula unlocked the passenger door, pushed down the seat, and tossed her pack to the far side of the back.

Cutty put her pack on the back seat. "I never knew that."

"One of the many things that makes the bug the coolest car ever," Paula said.

Cutty climbed into the tiny car as Paula went around to the driver's side and got in.

"It's so simple." Cutty studied the almost bare dashboard.

"Life used to be a lot simpler when this was built." Paula slipped the key into the ignition. She gave Cutty a giddy grin. "I loved this car." She turned the key, and the engine sputtered then purred to life.

"It lives," Cutty said.

"Chris really did take care of it. Hope I have a chance to thank her in person this trip." Paula put the car into gear and backed out of the spot.

Cutty couldn't help but let a bit of her own hidden hippie peek out.

Chapter 16

PAULA MARVELED AT how the atmosphere in Arcata hadn't changed, not to mention the sixties college-town feel of the neighborhood with several blocks of shops and restaurants where the Wildflower Café was located. They walked past a pair of gray-haired, shaggy-bearded hippies swapping stories in front of Big Pete's Pizza that had a mural of a baseball game painted on the wall on the neighboring wall. They passed three small houses and crossed the street to Wildflower Café, which was on the corner.

"This is it." Paula pushed open the door.

Cutty walked in, and Paula grinned at her nod of approval. The interior had a golden glow from the light-wood furniture and the sun slanting in through the side windows.

"Hi, sit anywhere." A thin, young woman with a long ponytail handed them menus.

They sat at a table in the back.

Paula looked at her watch. "David should be here soon."

"Hope he's figured out a way to get close to Strine," Cutty said.

The young woman approached their table. "Can I get you anything to drink?"

"Chai, please," Paula said.

Cutty nodded. "Sounds good."

The woman walked away. Paula looked around the half-filled establishment. Students worked on laptops and were reading while eating, professor-types engaged in conversation, local paintings on the walls and fresh-baked pastries and cookies filled the glass counter . . . a scene both familiar and comforting.

"It's that college nostalgia," Cutty said.

Paula blinked at her. "Huh?"

"Places like this"—Cutty glanced around—"bring out a nostalgia for all the good times you spent in places like this in college."

Paula chuckled. "In a way, we're no different than those aging hippies. We're just a couple of academics who are trying to survive outside of academia."

"I admit I think about getting a doctorate," Cutty said.

"That'd be fun." Paula looked at the menu. "Good. They still have the vegan mac and cheese. To die for."

"The jackfruit tacos sound good." Cutty put down her menu.

Paula looked up as the door opened. "That must be David."

A clean-cut young man in neat jeans and a navy-blue crew neck sweater with a light blue shirt and navy tie peeking up from the top of it walked in. He was either color challenged or his wife dressed him. Paula looked at his feet. At least he had on casual, comfortable-looking brown loafers.

The man looked around. Cutty held up a finger.

He nodded and walked to their table. "Cutty?"

"That's me," Cutty said. "This is Paula."

"Nice to meet both of you," David said.

Cutty gave him a smile. "Thank you for helping out with my case."

"It's not often I get to help with a murder that happened in Illinois," David said. "Mike speaks highly of you."

"He's a great guy," Cutty said.

Paula pushed out a chair for him. "We were about to order."

David sat down. "I was looking for an excuse to eat here."

"Go to school here?" Cutty handed him her menu.

"Yep. Fortuna's a half hour away, so I don't get up here that often for, shall we say, purely informational reasons." David nodded at the menu. "I love the avocado and cheese."

The young woman delivered the Chai teas and took their orders.

"So, do you have anything interesting for us?" Paula asked.

David turned on his tablet. "Ms. . . . Smith has lived in the area for six years. She has a house off one of the coastal roads north of Trinidad." He brought up a satellite map of Trinidad. "Off Stagecoach Road. A modest home by anyone's standards, much less a rock star."

Paula studied the map and noted the property was very close to the ocean. "Acreage?"

David gave her a quizzical look. "Thirty acres. Developers have shown great interest in taking some of it off her hands, but she's not interested in selling it. It goes up to the edge of the cliffs that overlook the beach."

"Does she have any out buildings, like a nice-looking barn?" Cutty asked.

David turned his quizzical gaze to her. "Yes. She built a really nice horse barn. The bottom level is made out of stone. The odd thing is—"

"She doesn't have any horses." Paula grinned as the young woman put a bowl of the vegan mac and cheese in front of her.

"Oh, wow." Cutty gazed at her tacos in delight. "Thank you."

"You're welcome." The young woman grinned as she put the avocado and cheese sandwich and a root beer in front of David. "Let me know of you need anything else."

Paula sampled a forkful. "This is great. Just as I remembered it."

"Ditto," Cutty mumbled around a mouthful.

David finished chewing and swallowing a bite. "Okay. Now you have me really curious. What's the deal with the barn? Does she have a killer drum set collection in there?"

Cutty put her fork down and turned to David. "She has a collection, all right." She leaned closer. "Ancient weapons."

David pulled back and blinked at her in surprise. "What?"

"She collects ancient weapons." Cutty dipped a chip into salsa.

David frowned. "Anything we have to worry about?"

Paula shook her head. "I'm sure she has them secure, given their value."

"Strange hobby," David muttered.

Paula and Cutty exchanged you-don't-know-the-half-of-it glances.

"So, how do we approach her without spooking her or having anyone else see us?" Cutty asked.

"I have to ask." David put down his sandwich. "Is she in some kind of trouble?"

Cutty shook her head. "We just need to get a piece of information to her and then meet with her to discuss this information."

David gave her a steady look and then took a sip of his root beer. "She's pretty comfortable driving around town and most people leave her alone. She goes to the restaurants, shops at Murphy's, walks on the beach . . ."

"What does she drive?" Cutty asked.

David pulled up a photo on his tablet.

Paula and Cutty looked at the vehicle and then at each other. They spluttered a laugh.

"We both lost big time on this one," Paula said.

"I certainly wouldn't have guessed a Toyota pickup," David said.

"At least it's black," Cutty said.

Paula turned to David. "We both guessed black."

"Why do you think she's being watch?" David asked.

"More like being kept an eye on. A little trickier because we don't know if someone is keeping an eye on her here." Paula cocked her head. "Why do you ask?"

David popped the last bite of his sandwich into his mouth and sorted through his photos as he chewed. He stopped on a nondescript black sedan.

"When I asked the Trinidad PD if they've seen anything out of the usual in relation to Ms. Smith, they had noted this car came into town the same day she had returned from her tour."

Cutty raised an eyebrow. "That's pretty observant, considering all the tourists in Trinidad."

David chuckled. "Well, normally they wouldn't have paid attention to it, but they found it parked on the road to her place. It's not unusual for cars to be parked on parts of the road because there are a couple of paths to the beach that are mostly known to the locals. But this car wasn't parked near any of these paths."

"Did they talk to the driver?" Paula asked.

"Yeah. They seemed to be tourists," David said. "A couple, maybe in their thirties. Fit, like hikers. They claimed they had heard about the beach trails and were trying to find one in the woods. The problem was, where they were, they'd run into the fence around Ms. Smith's property if they headed west."

"Was this the only time the sedan was around?" Paula asked.

David shook his head. "The couple checked into The Sea Shell, which is on Stagecoach Road within sight of the lane Ms. Smith lives on."

"Anything different about the couple . . . like their accent?" Paula asked.

"Yeah." David cocked his head. "The female's accent was Scottish or Irish."

"Have they done anything else suspicious?" Cutty asked.

"Well, they seem to be in close proximity to Ms. Smith a lot," David said.

Paula frowned. "Do they go into the shops or walk along the beach or put themselves in a position that they can be seen?"

"Yes to all." David rolled through his photographs. "After you contacted me, I went to investigate a bit. I found them in Murphy's Market."

"They were all in the store?" Cutty asked.

"Yes," David said. "Not only that but the couple weren't shy about letting Ms. Smith know they were there."

"Really?" Cutty responded as she exchanged glances with Paula.

David showed them a photo. Strine was at a deli counter, and the couple were at the end of the counter, watching her. Their expressions were a mix of amused teasing and taunting. The woman had her arms crossed like she was daring Strine to do something about them being there.

"They followed her like that as she shopped. Ms. Smith kept her expression stoic, but her body language showed her irritation." David looked up at them. "So does this make sense to you?"

"Believe it or not, it does," Cutty said. "Even better, you've given us the information we need to pursue our mission."

David gave her an amused look. "Are all unusual and unsolvable crimes so secretive?"

Paula grinned. "Of course. How else can they be unusual and unsolvable?"

Chapter 17

CUTTY AND PAULA sat in the VW Bug in a parking area on the spit of land that connected the tiny village of Trinidad with a craggy hill that reached out into the ocean and gazed at the water as it heaved in and out of an ever-changing mist.

"One thing that's been bothering me," Cutty said as she watched noisy sea gulls squabble over something.

Paula looked up from her work on an autograph book. "Only one thing?"

Cutty smirked. "Well, one major thing. If Strine's the boss, why doesn't she just tell her stalkers to leave her alone?"

Paula blinked at her. "Good question."

"And they certainly wouldn't be mocking her," Cutty said.

"On the other hand"—Paula closed the autograph book—"what can she do about them? She may be the boss but she can't fire them. They're most likely members of the League, which I would guess is hereditary."

"Kind of like family." Cutty stopped. "Family." She powered on her tablet and flipped through the photos David had given them. "How old do you think the woman is?" She handed the tablet to Paula.

Paula enlarged the photo of the female stalker in the deli and studied her face. "Early thirties, perhaps. Her hair is as black as Strine's. Same fair skin. Tall and lean like her."

"Sister? Cousin?"

Paula flashed her an impish look. "We'll have to remember to ask her."

"But"—Cutty sighed as her new theory deflated around her—"if she were her sister, she wouldn't be stalking her like that."

"It won't matter anyway if this doesn't work." Paula held up the autograph book. "Ready to show off your acting?"

Cutty laughed. "I'm always ready to show my ability to be a fan. Much easier than trying to act."

Paula handed her the book. "Good luck."

"Thanks." Cutty climbed out of the car, slung her little backpack over one shoulder, and walked to the sandy path. She took several steps in the soft mound of sand and almost lost her balance. She never thought walking on ocean sand would be so hard. She put her foot out and sank a little but slogged over the little mound to flatter, shallower ground.

Waves slapped the sand as Cutty walked toward the water to the ragged edge of a band of vegetation constantly reshaping by the rolling . . . noisy . . . and smelly ocean. She twitched her nose at the strong stench of fish and salt. She never expected the ocean to be so smelly or noisy.

She scooped up a few grains of the black sand. Paula said it was from all the volcanic activity around there.

She walked along, scanning the beach for interesting shells. As she knelt and picked up a rather beat-up sand dollar, she could see Strine walking her way from up the beach. Her stalkers were sauntering behind her and farther away from the water.

Cutty straightened and walked closer to the water's edge to pick up a shell with an orange tinge to it. *Okay. Relax. You're looking for shells. See her by accident when she's close enough to be recognized.* A good-sized shell winked at her in the foamy wash of the waves' edge. She squished through the water-packed sand and knelt down to look at the shell. She carefully lifted it from the sand, releasing a briny odor, and studied it with Strine in her line of sight. She pulled off her pack, took out a small towel, and wrapped the shell in it.

Strine stopped about ten feet away and scanned the misty ocean as if she had seen something.

Thank you, thank you. Cutty owed some deity big time. She looked up from her pack and blinked at Strine and then made sure her expression reflected a subdued recognition. She eagerly pulled the autograph book from her pack and stepped up to Strine as respectfully and unobtrusively as possible.

"Excuse me," she said in a quiet voice.

Strine turned her head, caught her eye, and looked down at the autograph book. She gave a grudging nod.

"Thank you." Cutty opened the book and handed it and a sharpie to Strine.

Strine stared at the opened book. Cutty prayed that the succinct wording on the page was enough to tell her that O'Hara knew they had the fragment when he had talked to her at the Portrait Gallery and that they just wanted to talk to her and return the fragment to her. A photograph of the fragment was on the opposite page.

Strine calmly turned the page and scribbled something that was more than her name. She closed the book and handed it and the Sharpie back to Cutty.

"Enjoy your visit to Trinidad." She gazed at Cutty, her deep green eyes both sad and enigmatic.

"Thank you." Cutty slipped the book into her pack. "For the autograph and your time."

Strine nodded and walked past her in the same unhurried manner.

Wow. Now that was acting.

Cutty was dying to know what Strine had written but continued to pretend to look for shells until Strine walked up to the parking area and her stalkers disappeared after her.

She faced the ocean, opened the backpack, and took out the book. She flipped to the page Strine had signed.

"Wow," she whispered.

Strine had written. "Make res at Larrupin for 6:30."

PAULA NAVIGATED THE dark and foggy Patrick's Point Road north of Trinidad. The road had an inn or cabins at every clearing in the woods, including the cabins they were staying in. Tall redwoods loomed up on either side of the road. Close to six-thirty felt like midnight with the sun setting at six o'clock that time of year.

"There it is." Cutty pointed as they came upon a clearing on the other side of the road. A two-story building with the bottom painted white and the top painted blue gray, stood back from the road with a pull-in parking area stretching for a small distance on either side of it. Only a handful of spaces were empty.

"Popular place." Paula turned into the space furthest from the door. "Don't see Strine's truck."

"She'll probably be fashionably late." Cutty opened her door and climbed out.

Paula pulled herself out of the bug and breathed in the cool, salty, moist air. Darkness added a special magic to the forest-ocean atmosphere.

They walked across the parking lot to the double glass doors, the gravel crunching below their shoes creating an unnatural disturbance in the country air.

"Love the fish." Cutty grinned at the sculpted red fish attached to the blue-gray brick above the door.

"At least it's not a wild goose." Paula pulled the door and held it open for Cutty.

Cutty shook her head as she walked through the doorway.

Paula followed her into a small and homey feeling dining room and went to the hostess stand. "Reservation for Downes." She thought it best not to use her name.

The woman crossed the name off her list and pulled several menus from the shelf.

"The third member of our party will be here soon," Paula said.

The woman smiled and nodded. "This way, please."

Paula took in the subdued olive green, unobtrusive paintings of still lifes, and red leather chairs that gave off a gentile, yet casual vibe. Most of the tables were occupied by what looked like locals with maybe some tourist types. The woman led them to a corner table that was as private as any table could be in the room.

They sat facing the other diners. The last thing they wanted was an unexpected, possibly unpleasant surprise.

Cutty opened the menu. Her eyebrows shot up. "Glad this is on the company dime."

Paula looked at the menu. "Pricey, but it's supposed to be good."

"They have some vegetarian options," Cutty said.

"Welcome to California." Paula grinned. She looked up at a movement near the door. Strine, clad in what Paula could only call rich casual—jeans, russet flannel shirt, and brown leather jacket—was talking to the hostess.

Cutty exchanged looks with Paula. "Wonder how she shook her stalkers."

Paula gave her an amused look. "She *can* pop in and out of caves."

The hostess, clutching a menu, led Strine to their table.

Strine nodded to them, pulled out a chair, and sat down. She accepted the menu. "Thank you."

The hostess smiled and walked away. Obviously, Strine was a known entity in this establishment.

Strine gazed at Paula and Cutty with impassive eyes, the green almost gray in the dim light.

"I'm Paula Reisling," Paula said. "And this is Cutty Downes."

"Cutty." Strine's eyes twinkled. "I like that."

"Short for Cuthbertson," Cutty said.

A server approached the table. "Would you like something to drink?"

Strine turned to her. "A moonstone, please."

"Elk River," Cutty said.

"Make that two." Paula always liked sampling the local brew.

"I'll be right back with your drinks." The server gave Strine a smile and walked away.

"I'm the police chief of Licking Creek, Illinois," Cutty said.

"And I'm the Director of the Repository of Unusual Unsolvable Crimes," Paula said.

Strine let out a quiet laugh and shook her head. "And I seem to be the bloody idiot in the middle."

Paula shrugged. "Well, I prefer the word mystery."

The server delivered their ales and took their orders.

"What is that?" Cutty stared at the black liquid with a thin brown head in Strine's pint glass.

"A local porter." Strine took a sip. "It's rather an acquired taste."

"I bet," Cutty muttered.

Cutty took a sip of her amber ale and nodded her approval. "First off, we want you to know, given the nature of this, uh, situation, we can't apprehend or even detain you. Let's just say this case has very special evidentiary circumstances."

Strine emitted a gentle snort of amusement. "I'm already imprisoned in my own failure."

Paula glanced at Cutty, who shrugged. "That's why we're here. We could have just given up when we realized we couldn't bring this case to a legal conclusion. But we realized you need to restore your honor, and O'Hara has been keeping things from you."

Strine's eyes widened in surprise.

"I think we'll just tell you what we know . . . from the beginning."

As they ate, Cutty, with Paula's help, told Strine everything from discovering the crime scene to O'Hara stealing the fragment. Strine's eyes hardened into a carefully controlled anger during that part of the story and her laugh of delight at their letting the air out of O'Hara's tires and delivering the pizzas to his room seemed to show they were gaining her trust.

"That brings us up to now," Paula said. "We know that only you can restore the sword."

Strine took a sip of her after dinner tea with milk. "Well, I guess I got lucky that you decided to pursue this case." She straightened. "I have several problems with fixing my problem."

"O'Hara," Cutty said.

"And you know he doesn't know how to restore the sword," Paula said.

"Exactly." Strine looked into her tea cup.

Paula felt a vibration in her jacket pocket. She pulled out her phone. Her tracer on Strine's stalkers was moving. "Your shadows are on the move."

Strine squinted at the phone. "You're tracking them?"

"Yep."

The little green blip headed south on Stagecoach Road into Trinidad.

"Think they know you gave them the slip?" Cutty asked.

"Even if they did, they couldn't find me," Strine said. "I keep a car at a neighbor's house. I cut through my property to their place."

"They don't seem to be doubling back to get on Patrick's Point Road," Cutty said as the blip went past the road that cut up to where they were.

The blip entered the town, turned east on Main Street, and went through town to 101.

"Where're they going?" Strine muttered.

The green blip rolled off the highway a few miles south of Trinidad.

"That's the casino," Strine said.

"They like to gamble?" Cutty asked.

Strine gave them a wry look. "I wouldn't doubt it."

Time for some data mining. "Don't feel highly about them?" Paula asked.

Strine sat back and stared at the green blip, now stopped in the casino parking lot. "Alys is my cousin. She's"—She sat up and took a sip of tea—"O'Hara's daughter."

"O'Hara's your uncle?" Cutty leaned forward on the table.

"My late mother's brother." Strine looked up at them. "We're a matriarchal society. The power is passed from daughter to daughter."

"So how is O'Hara the keeper of the sword?" Paula asked.

Strine rested weary eyes on her. "Unprecedented circumstances." She shifted her gaze to the tablecloth. "Everything about this is unprecedented. It's like we're being punished for allowing a man to do women's work." She lifted her eyes. "I keep thinking the sword wouldn't have broken if it had been in a woman's care."

A profound sadness crept over Paula. A long proud tradition had been all but destroyed even before Strine popped into the cave in Illinois. "Do you think he has kept his knowledge of us and the fragment from you because he wants to prove he should be the keeper?"

Strine stared at the tablecloth for a few moments, then nodded. "He has always been too . . . male . . . for the job. Too much ego."

"Do you have the power to remove him from the position?" Cutty asked.

Strine rested her eyes on her. "I'm surprised the League hasn't raised an inquiry about the . . . failure."

Cutty and Paula exchanged glances.

"We believe O'Hara hasn't told anyone other than the blacksmith," Cutty said. "That he told them the mission was a success and the sword is safely where it's supposed to be."

Strine slowly nodded. "That makes sense . . . and explains why I haven't been called in to . . . make a report."

"Would O'Hara have told his daughter?" Paula asked.

Strine blinked up at her. "She doesn't *need* a reason to harass me. He most likely told her to keep an eye on me, but this feeds into her ambition, too. So I don't know."

"What about her . . . ?"

"Husband?" Strine snorted. "A weak puppy. Just Alys's type."

Paula gave herself a decisive nod. "This started out as just a case for us, but it's turned into an incredible quest. We seriously want to see this to the end. To see your honor restored and O'Hara getting his just desserts." She gave Cutty a questioning look. Cutty nodded with eager excitement in her eyes. "So will you allow us to join forces with you to restore your sword and your tradition of saving the world."

Strine stared at them in astonishment.

Paula put out her fist. Cutty hit Paula's fist with her own and held it out.

Strine gazed at the fists and raised her eyes. They were filled with intrigue and a hint of something Paula had yet to see in those amazing green eyes. Hope.

Strine bumped her fist against Cutty's and Paula's. "*Fuil gaiscioch deo.* Blood hero forever."

Part III

When the Unsolvable Meets the Unassailable

Chapter 18

"THE PLACE IS busy." Cutty gazed at the rows of cars as Paula drove up and down the aisles of the casino parking lot in search of an empty space.

"It's Friday night." Paula pulled into an empty spot in the aisle as far away from the casino as they could get. "Not much else to do around here."

She grabbed a backpack from the back seat and rummaged through it. She took out a tube of hair gel. "Fauxhawk, spiked, or fashionable disarray?"

"Hmmm." Cutty studied Paula. "It's a casino. Maybe fashionable disarray. You want to be in disguise, not bring attention to yourself."

Paula rubbed gel on her hands and ran them through her hair into a messy doo. She then exchanged her wire rims for black plastic glasses. "How do I look?"

Cutty gazed at her. "Eerily like Buddy Holly. Kind of spooky actually."

"We nerds are all siblings by different earthlings." Paula grinned. "Do I look like me?"

"Weirdly, no." Cutty shook her head. "That's an amazing talent."

"Comes in handy at Halloween parties." Paula opened her door, letting in moist, much colder air.

Cutty climbed out of the car and looked past the rows of cars at the Cher-au Heights Casino up the hill. The colorfully lit building was different sized Indian lodges built on several levels of ground. Quaint looking by casino standards.

Paula stepped up next to her. "Okay. Let's see what the stalkers are up to."

They walked between parked cars up the gentle slope of the hill to a set of steps cut into a stone wall that went to the top of a semi-circle driveway. Cutty wasn't sure if she really wanted all that extra cardio after a rich meal.

"I've never been in a casino before." She looked across the driveway at the banks of sparkling, colorful slot machines through the glass doors.

"They have lots of flashing lights, loud cartoon noises, and smoke," Paula said.

Cutty wrinkled her nose. "Smoke?"

"Tribes are allowed to set their own smoking laws," Paula said.

"Great," Cutty muttered as they crossed the driveway. The glass doors flowed open and the dinging and clattering of slot machines flowed out, not to mention the stench of cigarette smoke. "That's a blast from the past I don't miss at all."

"Could be worse," Paula said as they walked through the doorway. "Not as many people smoke nowadays."

Cutty fought back a sneeze. "I'll try not to breathe in too deeply."

"Let's mosey around, like we're looking for an interesting slot machine." Paula nodded at a row of slots against a wall.

Cutty stared at the machines based on television shows and movies. She had no idea they were so commercial. Not many people were at the slots, and the space was small enough for them to walk around it in a few minutes.

Paula stopped and stared at the instructions on a machine with a fantasy theme.

"Any ideas?" Cutty asked.

"If they're meeting someone, they wouldn't be in a gaming room." Paula looked up. "I think we need a drink before we try a slot machine."

Cutty raised an eyebrow.

"Over there." Paula nodded at a pair of glass doors with Firestarter Lounge written in fiery neon letters above them.

"Sounds like a good idea."

They walked into the spacious high-ceiling bar. Most of the tables were full of noisy people who weren't there for meaningful discussions on the mysteries of life. A long bar lined the far wall with every seat taken.

They walked toward an empty table near the small, thankfully empty stage. The bar was noisy enough from the blasting sound system and patrons shouting their conversations.

"I don't see them," Paula said.

"Just as well." Cutty skirted around the tables and people toward the door. "It's too noisy in here."

Cutty pushed opened the glass door and stepped into the main room with relief. The concentration of noise and smoke set her on edge.

"What about there?" She nodded at a sign for the Sunrise Deli.

Paula shrugged. "Why not?"

They walked past banks of ear-splitting slot machines to the mercifully quiet deli. Half the tables were occupied with people who looked as if they were refueling after gambling too much.

Paula nodded at the corner next to the bank of windows where the stalkers were digging into ice cream sundaes and looking none too happy. She led the way to a table next to the wall with a clear view of them.

Cutty sat against the wall, facing the stalkers, pulled out her phone, and stuck her Bluetooth receiver into her ear.

Paula leaned on the table with both hands. "Want some ice cream?"

"Sure." Cutty brought up her spy program and grinned at Paula. "Surprise me."

Paula waggled her eyebrows and walked to the counter.

Cutty pulled off her baseball cap, attached her peace symbol button with the tiny camera on its front, and put the cap back on. The stalkers appeared on the phone screen.

" . . . even here anyway." Alys's husband's sullen voice came through clearly in Cutty's ear.

"Plans have changed," Alys said in an irritated tone, as if she'd been repeating it all night.

They then worked on their sundaes in silence.

Cutty wondered who they were talking about. She couldn't imagine the changed plans being in Strine's favor.

A phone chirped. Cutty jumped.

Alys held her phone to her ear. "We're waiting." She listened for a few seconds. "Okay. We're in the Sunrise Deli."

Paula approached with two hot fudge sundaes. "I decided to go traditional." She put the sundaes on the table and sat opposite Cutty.

"Perfect," Cutty said. "Whoever they're waiting for is going to show up soon. All I've learned is plans have changed."

Paula looked up from dipping her spoon in the ice cream. "That doesn't sound good." She pulled her Bluetooth from her pocket and pressed it into her ear.

The stalkers ate in silence, neither looking happy to be there just waiting. Talkative, Cutty mused as she zoomed the camera for a closer view of them.

"They have a four hundred seat bingo room." Paula looked up from the brochure she was reading. "That explains why the parking lot is full."

"Bingo?" The image of seniors in a church basement flashed through Cutty's mind. She caught a movement at the door. O'Hara, dressed down in a preppy blue polo and khaki slacks and navy sports jacket, scanned the room, saw Alys, and walked to her table.

"Daddy, dear," Cutty mumbled.

Paula opened a brochure about Patrick's Point State Park. "To quote Alice, curiouser and curiouser."

O'Hara sat at the table, providing Cutty with a side view of him.

"Good evening, daughter," he said in a tight, formal tone.

Paula raised an eyebrow at Cutty. Cutty hid her amusement by digging up a scoop of ice cream. Great family dynamics.

"Father," Alys said in an emotionless voice.

O'Hara took Alys's hand. "You've done yourself proud in fulfilling this mission."

Alys stared at him and gave a quick nod. "*Teughlach an chéad.*"

"Family first." O'Hara squeezed her hand then released it. He pulled something from his jacket pocket and put it on the table. A slender black box maybe ten inches long. "I revisited a passage in the ancient text that I had thought curious when I first read it. I compared the translation to modern Irish with the original text and found a point of ambiguity, but in context, the alternative interpretation made more sense than the translation." He captured Alys's eyes. "Our ancestors weren't ones to write in parables and riddles. Our charge is a serious one, and they had to be as clear as possible in their instructions."

"Then why did the translators choose the alternative that made less sense?" Alys asked.

"Because"—O'Hara sighed in a manner as measured as his words— "the translators always erred in favor of the swordbearer."

Paula looked up from the brochure, her eyes reflecting the chill that went down Cutty's spine.

Alys's eyes glinted with cold anticipation.

Cutty's chill turned into a shudder. Alys appeared to be a chip off the old ice block.

"Up to now, we thought the ancient texts did not address the possibilities of failure," O'Hara said.

"And now?" Alys's eagerness was both intense and frightening.

"It seems that if the swordbearer fails, the next in line must take her place," O'Hara said.

Alys stared at him as if processing his words. "What about the sword?"

"Because she failed, she can't fix it." O'Hara's smug grin was both triumphant and hideous. "But you can."

"The swordbearer can't be killed," Alys said.

"Every weapon can be disarmed." A half smile touched O'Hara's lips. "The swordbearer can be killed by the steel of her own sword."

Alys slumped her shoulders. "Which is missing."

"I said the *steel*."

Alys narrowed her eyes. "The fragment you no longer have."

"We've not only preserved the sword through the ages, we've preserved a small ingot of the same alloy." O'Hara put two fingers on the black box. "All you need for the job is here."

Alys gazed at the box. She lifted the hinged lid with long delicate fingers and stared at a dagger that looked like a miniature sword.

"I had Ferguson forge it into an appropriate weapon for our future swordbearer." O'Hara gazed at her with a fierce eagerness.

"And how do I perform the deed?"

O'Hara shrugged. "You've been following her around easily enough. It shouldn't be hard to find the opportunity in such a remote wooded area as this, to do your mischief."

Alys ran her finger over the blade. "And then what?"

"We get the fragment from our favorite archivist and reforge the sword," O'Hara said.

Paula's eyes twinkled in amusement.

Alys looked up with a disdain that showed she wasn't above calling her father a failure. "You already tried that."

O'Hara's flash of irritation faded into an evil triumphant grin. "I figured out the swordbearer is the only one who can restore a sword. *That's* why we didn't succeed."

Alys grinned, a wicked hideous glint in her eyes as she closed the lid on the box. "*Fuil gaisioch deo.*"

O'Hara straightened, pride in his eyes. "*Fuil gaisioch deo.*"

"I'LL EXPLAIN EVERYTHING," Cutty said into her phone. "Just get out of there."

Paula glanced at her as she followed Alys's black car around the back of the casino to the Oceanside road to Trinidad.

"Go to the Sea Cliff Motel on Patrick's Point. Number four. See you soon." Cutty disconnected.

The black sedan turned onto Main Street, and Paula continued across the intersection to Patrick's Point Road.

"Okay, we can get Alys and her weirdly passive husband on breaking and entering." Paula watched for the motel's entrance in the dark trees.

"Fortunately, a sheriff's deputy is close enough to catch them just as they break in. That ought to give us some time to plan."

"Do you think O'Hara has figured it out?" Cutty asked.

"Seriously?" Paula saw the sign for the Sea Cliff Motel and pulled into the gravel lot alongside a quaint white building and several cabins. "I think he's doing everything he can to make his little girl swordbearer. He's going to interpret those ancient texts any way that gets him to that goal."

"I do think he's right that Strine figured out she's the only one who can restore the sword," Cutty said.

Paula parked in front of number four. "Let's just hope she has some ideas about what she's supposed to do."

"Amen to that." Cutty climbed out of the car.

Paula eased out of the bug and looked out toward the road. Dark and quiet. She followed Cutty to the cabin door.

Cutty opened the door and a blast of warmth hit them. "Guess we left the heater on."

Paula laughed as she walked in and turned down the freestanding room heater. A bed in a wood bed frame and country quilt was up against one wall and a matching daybed was next to the opposite wall. A nice cozy place she wouldn't mind spending a few days in . . . she didn't even stop herself from adding, with Cutty. The fun, flirty vibe between them had become a natural part of their banter.

Cutty went through an open doorway in the back into the kitchen.

Headlights flashed through the room. Paula opened the front door as a small, dark blue car parked in front of the cabin. Strine unfolded herself out of the car.

"That's the best disguise I've ever seen," Paula said.

Strine gave her a blank look, then looked at the car, and laughed. "No one looks twice at a Honda Fit and would never expect someone six-one to be driving it."

"Brilliant." Paula stepped aside, and Strine walked past her into the cabin.

"I'm making a pot of tea," Cutty said from the kitchen.

"We've got quite a story for you," Paula said as they sat around the woodblock table in the tiny, but quaintly decorated kitchen.

Cutty picked up the ceramic teapot with ducks on it and poured tea into mismatched mugs, while Paula powered up the laptop on the table. She brought up the video stream they had taken at the casino. Brie had been burning the midnight oil—probably watching a horror movie marathon—to be awake to upload the video to the cloud.

Strine looked up from mixing sugar and milk into her tea. "O'Hara has never come out here. He's an east coast snob. One of the reasons I chose the remotest part of California for my refuge."

"Well, double thumbs up on your choice," Paula said. "I love it up here."

"I'll be glad to get back to being left alone."

Paula exchanged looks with Cutty.

"You might be able to take care of your problems once and for all," Cutty said.

Strine frowned. "Why?"

Paula pushed play on the video.

Strine watched the video impassively. Only a cold cast to her eyes when O'Hara revealed what he was up to betrayed her seething anger.

They sat in silence when the video was finished, the shadow of menacing violence out of place in the cheery country-style kitchen.

Strine finally sucked in a deep breath and took a sip of her tea. "We've been lucky through all these centuries that a swordbearer and the keeper have been direct heirs. Sisters. Several sisters for many generations. My sister . . ." She stared at the far wall.

Paula and Cutty stayed still, willing Strine to tell her story.

Strine returned her attention to her mug of tea. "My sister died under mysterious circumstances." She looked up. "Of course, it was ruled a tragic accident, and I thought no differently at the time. She was a daredevil—like most of my kin—it's something that's in our blood. The legend is we're all weaned on *briana laochra ar*—warrior's milk. She was sixteen and was hang-gliding in Ireland with some friends . . . and Alys. Everyone except for Alys and Aine, my sister, had taken off, so Alys was the only eyewitness to what had happened." She drained her tea.

Cutty poured more tea into Strine's mug.

Strine gave her a small smile of thanks. "Alys said that Aine took off next, and the canopy collapsed when she was airborne." She focused on pouring milk and sugar into her tea. "She crashed into the cliff face."

"And what made you change your mind about what happened?" Cutty asked softly.

Strine captured Cutty's eyes. "A few years later, when I was sixteen, the clan gathered to observe Beltane. We met at a family lodge in the Appalachians. Most of the clan had settled in America by then. It's near a particularly scenic and dramatic part of the Appalachian trail, and we liked to hike it. I woke up early one clear, beautiful morning and decided to go up to a point along the trail that had a good view of the sunrise." She sipped her tea.

Paula sat forward in anticipation. Cutty flashed her a look. They both seemed to realize that, while Strine was a hero-murderer, her cousin was a ruthless monster.

"I sat on the rock, enjoying the cool air and the peace." Strine's face softened. "I'd been watching sunrises from that spot since I was twelve. It was kind of my special thing to do. The sun was just visible over a peak across the valley, and I heard someone coming up the path below. I thought it was just a hiker and didn't pay them any attention. Then I heard Alys say, 'So this is where you go in the morning.' She was standing behind me. The perch is a roundish flat rock, maybe six feet in diameter. I was irritated that she found me. She never let me enjoy anything."

"That explains her outright taunting you," Cutty said.

Strine nodded. "That's the way she's always behaved toward me." She pulled a cookie out of the opened bag on the table and nibbled it—her expression thoughtful and resolved. "I looked back at Alys, and she had a look in her eyes. Just a glint, but it scared me. It was so cold, so cruel. She came up behind me and put her hands on my shoulders, harder than necessary. I knew not to say something like, 'let go.' She'd only taunt me for being weak, or worse, afraid. She pushed, not hard enough to push me off the rock. I used my strength to barely budge. She gave a laugh and let go of my shoulders. 'You know, it can be dangerous here alone,' she said. I looked back at her and said, 'Sometimes even more dangerous when I'm not alone.' I held her eyes long enough for her to know that I knew what she was thinking of doing." She raised her eyes. "Because at that moment I put together all her taunts about how Aine had been weak and didn't have what it took to be a swordbearer and how Alys was the only one who knew what had happened to Aine."

"So, the unprecedented circumstances?" Paula asked.

Strine blinked at her and then nodded. "When the swordbearer, my mother, died, I was the only female in the line. By tradition the swordbearer chooses her keeper—we usually have several aunts and sisters to choose from. I chose my mother's keeper—her cousin—Morrigan, who has three fine daughters." She focused on them. "If I die without a female heir, the swordbearer line goes to the keeper."

"So what happened?" Cutty pulled a cookie from the bag.

"Uncle Seamus challenged it," Strine said. "He remembered an account of a story about an underage swordbearer. The ancient texts said she could not choose her keeper, that the keeper must come from the line of her next of kin, even if the head of that line is a male, as long as he had a daughter. The thing is we've never had a male keeper, so he explained, a sister, who everyone thought had been dead turned out to be alive in this story."

"Convenient," Paula said.

"Morrigan said she couldn't find anything about the story in the ancient texts. Uncle Seamus said he found the story in one of our histories. It's in Old Irish, so its translation can be interpreted different ways. But Seamus had studied ancient languages in college, and Morrigan learned them in the traditional way of the clan. Seamus gave his case that he had formally studied ancient languages because we had strayed too far from the original meaning of the text. Implying that the text as an oral tradition, not the ability to read it, had been passed down through the generations. In the end, he convinced the League he was correct about the underage story."

"You mean Morrigan just gave up her keepership?" Cutty asked.

Strine shrugged, resigned. "You have to understand the dynamics of the League."

"I take it O'Hara's the only one allowed to see these ancient texts." Paula sat back and contemplated the clock on the wall. Only a quarter past midnight.

"Right," Strine said.

"Do you know where these texts are kept?" Paula asked.

"In the vault, where the sword is kept," Strine said. "I know the location, but not how to get into it."

Paula tucked that info in the back of her mind for now. "And you were underage when your mother died?"

"Just shy of my eighteenth birthday," Strine said.

Paula raised an eyebrow. "How convenient."

Strine gave her a don't-I-know-it look.

"So"—Cutty sat forward and put her elbows on the table—"what was the age of adulthood twenty-five hundred years ago?"

Strine gazed at her for several seconds, opened her mouth and then closed it. She sat back, looking a little stunned.

"Can we talk to Morrigan?" Paula asked.

Strine slowly nodded. "She removed herself and her daughters from the clans, and now lives near Port Angeles, Washington."

Cutty's phone chirped. She looked at the number. Humboldt County police. She put it on speaker. "Downes."

"Chief Downes, this is Deputy Cobbs. We apprehended three intruders trying to break into Strine's home. We waited until they set off the alarm before moving in, as you requested. They didn't take or break anything."

"Good work," Cutty said. "Were they armed?"

"The older man, a Seamus O'Hara, had a pistol," Deputy Cobbs said. "The woman, Alys O'Hara, had a small dagger."

"Interesting," Cutty said. "Hold them for as long as you can for us."

"Will do," Deputy Cobbs said.

Cutty disconnected and looked at Strine. "You can't press charges because you have to stay under their radar until we can fight back. I suggest we go to your place so you can secure what needs to be secured and pack for an interesting road trip."

"Not quite how I planned to spend my break away from the band." Strine chuckled. "But if we can remove Uncle Seamus and Alys from the League and restore the traditions to the way they're supposed to be, I'd hop a shuttle to the moon if necessary."

Chapter 19

AS MUCH AS she missed the VW bug, Cutty had to admit Strine's truck made the trip through Oregon a lot more comfortable. She took in the passing countryside, gray and overcast—although she had heard summers in the Northwest were beautiful and sunny. She'd have to come back in the summer and do the trip on the coast instead of boring Interstate 5. She grinned as she glanced behind her, where Paula was sprawled in the back, dead to the world. Maybe she could talk her into coming along.

Strine, stretched out in the passenger seat, shifted a bit but didn't wake up.

Cutty was glad she got some sleep last night, while Paula and Strine went to Strine's house to get whatever she needed for the trip and to secure the house, leave the Bug, and grab the truck. That morning, they stopped at the Humboldt County Sheriff's Office in Eureka, where O'Hara, Alys, and her weirdly passive husband were cooling their heels in the lockup.

Cutty went into the facility to examine the dagger and take pictures of it. She also slipped trackers under the ornamental extension over the blade and into the hems of Alys's and O'Hara's coats.

After eight hours of driving with brief stops for gas—who knew Oregon didn't have self-serve gas—and food, Cutty was ready to turn the wheel over to whoever wanted it.

A bleary-eyed Paula appeared in the rearview mirror. She put on her glasses and blinked out the window.

"Portland," Cutty said. "If this is the traffic on a Saturday at five, I'd hate to see it during rush hour."

"At least it's moving." Paula pushed a hand through her hair. "Let's get over the river and look for a place to eat in Vancouver."

"River?"

"The Columbia," Paula said.

"Seriously?" Cutty bubbled with excitement. "Like Lewis and Clark?"

"Yes." Paula grinned. "The Columbia River is the border between Oregon and Washington."

"Wow, I never knew that."

Strine pulled herself up and blinked out the window. "Where'd all the cars come from?"

"Portland," Cutty said.

They went through some tunnels and the buildings of downtown Portland loomed ahead.

"The biggest city I've ever driven in is St. Louis." Cutty took deep breaths to stay calm.

"Just keep track of the lanes for 5 north," Paula said. "Don't panic, just ease yourself into the lanes if you need to."

Cutty pushed down her panic as a ramp full of cars converged and peeled off lanes on both sides of her. Five north. Five north. Five . . . She saw the sign and was relieved she was in the correct lane. She kept focused on the signs and the vehicles in front of her, just registering the spaghetti bowl of lanes crisscrossing at different angles around and below her. Just as she merged with lanes of traffic coming up on her left, she was over water.

"Is this the Columbia?" she asked.

"The Willamette," Paula said. "It splits Portland in two."

The highway hugged the edge of the river as they flowed along in the heavy traffic toward the tall buildings of downtown.

"Okay." Paula looked around. "You're doing great. Should be easier now."

"Thanks." Cutty eased up on clutching the steering wheel.

"Portland's an interesting place," Strine said. "Very laid back, into everything alternative. Good concert crowd."

Cutty glanced at her. "Bet you don't see much of the places you play at."

Strine chuckled. "We're lucky to know what town we're in."

The traffic thinned, and they moved smoothly past tall walls on either side of the highway with the occasional hint of buildings on top of rises in the land. They crossed over a narrow channel of water.

"We're actually on a big island in the Columbia River," Paula said.

"Really?" Cutty looked around. "Wow."

Marinas appeared, and they rolled over a wider band of water. Then they come upon a green metal trestle covering the roadway.

"Wow, just this part is wider than the Mississippi," Cutty said as she glanced around at the river.

Paula grinned. "Welcome to Washington state." She looked down at her phone. "I think there are places to eat up here. We need a bit of a breather."

"I need a breather." Cutty gave her an amused look in the rearview mirror. "You need caffeine so you can drive."

"And it's getting dark already." Paula looked up. "Okay, there're several restaurants nearby. Get off at the 78th Street exit."

Cutty navigated off the highway to a shopping center parking lot and pulled in front of what looked like a very popular fast food Mexican place on the corner. She got out of the car and stretched her stiff legs. The sky was almost completely dark, despite being only six in the evening, and considerably cooler than Trinidad.

"Toss out my jacket," she said to Paula as Paula climbed out of the back.

Paula grabbed Cutty's jacket, handed it to her, and slipped on her own jacket.

"Thanks," Cutty said.

Strine pulled on a baseball hat. She looked very un-rock star like with a maroon crew neck sweater under her black leather jacket and worn jeans. She also had on wire rim glasses that made her look geeky enough to not bring attention to herself. Another person who could disguise themselves without really trying. Cutty couldn't help but feel a little envious of this skill.

The restaurant was full of people forming what looked like chaotic lines in front of the service counter. Cutty kept reminding herself that it was Saturday night and most people had real lives.

"I'll snag a table." She scanned the menu board on the wall. "I'll have a grilled veggie burrito. And a coke."

Paula nodded. "Got it."

Cutty spotted a table near the wall and grabbed it. She pulled out her phone and checked their trackers. They were still blipping together but were back in Trinidad. Someone must have posted bail for them. She zoomed in on the blips. They seemed to be outside Strine's house.

Paula approached the table with their drinks. Her long fingers easily wrapped around the three-cup triangle. "Strine's in the john."

She sat down and pushed a cup to Cutty and toward an empty chair.

"They're out of jail." Cutty showed Paula her phone.

Paula picked up the phone and played with the zoom. "They think she's home."

"And they're waiting for her to come out of the house." Cutty frowned. "How long do you think it'll be before they realize she's not there?"

Paula shook her head as she put the phone on the table. "I hope long enough for us to figure out what we're doing."

Cutty watched Strine push around the tables full of people. She wore an impassive expression, as if eating at a fast-food Mexican restaurant in Vancouver, Washington was something she did every day.

Cutty wondered what her life had been like growing up. Now she was rich and famous, but had she always been rich? O'Hara certainly didn't give the impression of being anything less than upper crust. Strine had the unforced air of someone brought up to have manners and a good education. And it wasn't just the compelling Irish lilt to her speech.

Strine sat down and took a sip of her drink. She gazed at the phone. "Looks like they're out."

"And outside your house." Paula stood. "That's our number." She went to the food counter.

"When will they suspect you're not there?" Cutty asked.

Strine chuckled. "Until they think I'm out of food." She smiled as Paula put a basket of food in front of each of them and another full of chips in the middle of the table. "I've spent my career as a swordbearer reminding him of his place."

Cutty stuck a fork into her messy burrito. "What does the rest of the League think of his superior attitude?"

Strine swallowed a mouthful of taco. "They don't like it, but they can't interfere between the swordbearer and the keeper unless tenets have been broken."

"Which they have," Paula said.

"But the League doesn't know that," Strine said.

"And you haven't told them because they would find out about your failure," Cutty said.

Strine gazed at her with thoughtful eyes tinged with sadness. "Initially, yes. But now . . ." She took a deep breath. "Now, after talking with you, I'm waiting until I prove O'Hara's failure as a keeper."

She put her hand on her front jean pocket and pulled out her phone. Cutty saw an image of a Celtic knot around a sword instead of a photo of a person displayed.

"O'Hara." She pushed "answer" and put the phone to her ear and listened. "Get away from my property." She listened some more and rolled her eyes at Cutty and Paula. "I'm not interested in talking to you."

Strine's impatience sparked in her eyes, even as she kept her expression even. She barked a laugh. "You're ordering me? You forget. Only I can give the orders. And I order you to get away from my property and out of Trinidad." She disconnected the call.

"Where would they think you went if they figure out you're not home?" Paula asked.

Strine munched a chip as she thought. "I really don't know. Something like this has never happened before."

"Would he think you'd go to his predecessor?"

Strine shrugged. "I think he'd consider it."

Cutty stuck her fork into her burrito. "Then we'll just have to get there first."

PAULA HAD TO rely completely on GPS because the darkness not only hid building and street signs but all sense of direction. Remote didn't even begin to describe this part of Washington.

"I haven't been here in a long time," Strine said. "We just came off of a world tour."

Cutty gave her a sidelong look. "Will she be happy to see us?"

Strine chuckled. "She'll be ecstatic to see us and appalled at the reason we're here."

"As long as she can help us." Cutty poked her head between the front seats.

Strine stared at the road, illuminated by the truck headlights and surrounded by deep blackness. "I always got the impression that something was . . . not right . . . but my aunt couldn't say anything. She was no longer the keeper of the sword and she was not allowed to speak of the knowledge she had."

"What about now?" Cutty asked. "Considering that's why we're here."

Shrine turned to Cutty. "The current keeper has failed and it's possible he doesn't know what to do." She shrugged. "All bets are off. It's up to me to restore order to our traditions and get the sword back. My aunt will do as I ask, because I shall select her as my new keeper."

"As simple as that?" Paula asked.

"I've realized that I am without a keeper right now," Strine said. "It's now clear I never had one, because O'Hara can't perform his duty. He has been a pretender and the consequence has been a destruction of our purpose."

Paula peered at an intersection with a gas station on the corner. "I turn right here?"

"Yes," Strine said. "Follow the road to the end."

Paula turned onto a narrow blacktop. Lights in windows of houses sparkled on the hill behind rows of mailboxes next to narrow dirt or gravel lanes every once in a while as they plowed through the darkness. They were definitely climbing as the turns sharpened and the mailboxes and lanes lined only one side. Up ahead stood a wood barrier and a sign warning them that they were at a dead end.

"Follow the track on the left," Strine said.

Paula peered to the left and saw only darkness. She maneuvered the truck to the side, and the headlights illuminated a very narrow dirt and gravel track, more suitable for tractors than cars.

"Glad we have a truck," she muttered as she eased the vehicle into the deep, uneven ruts.

They bumped along into a forest of trees that threatened to engulf the track before they went around a sharp curve. Metal gates attached to formidable stone pillars loomed ahead.

"Now, why wasn't I expecting this?" Cutty asked, wryly.

Strine flashed a grin. "Pull up to the gate."

Paula crept the truck forward. The gate slid as a single piece into one of the stone pillars.

"Cool," Cutty said.

"I thought you didn't contact her," Paula said.

Strine gazed ahead with an amused look. "I didn't."

"And why am I not surprised she knew to open the gate before we had a chance to talk into that little box?" Cutty said.

Paula could only shake her head as she drove between the pillars. She looked in the rearview mirror. The gate was already half-closed.

The track took another sharp turn and became black as pitch.

"What the—?" Paula rolled the car onto a smooth surface. "Ah, paved."

"My aunt likes to discourage people from wandering onto her property," Strine said.

"You think?" Cutty chuckled.

Paula steered the truck around several more curves, all the time climbing. A tall wood sculpture loomed to the right in a small clearing in the dense trees. It looked like a dragon totem. Warning or welcome?

A well-constructed wall of field stone maybe seven or eight feet high stood across the road.

Paula put on the brakes and turned to Strine. "What now?"

Strine grinned. "Just wait."

Paula stared at the wall and blinked. Did something move? A slab of stones pivoted on an off-centered point, leaving a blank space in the wall. Another slab of stones pivoted, enlarging the black gap wide enough for them to drive through.

Paula gave Strine a wry look. "You guys could clean up designing theme parks."

Strine laughed. "Necessity is the mother of invention."

Paula drove through the gap and saw lights flickering in the distance. A house at last? The lights coalesced into glows through metal stencils shaped like Celtic knots embedded in field stone pillars on either side of the road and lining a sizable cobblestone semi-circle in front of a log structure on top of a rough stone foundation. The building looked like a small vacation lodge with three stories and veranda wings that wrapped partially around the stone courtyard.

"Wow," Cutty said. "Looks like my dream home."

Strine grinned at her. "It used to be a resort but was in disrepair when my aunt bought it. She loves to putter around, fixing and building things."

"Where do I park?" Paula peered around the empty drive.

"Anywhere." Strine waved forward. "Close to the front door."

Paula pulled up to the side of a wide set of steps that cascaded down from the veranda and shut off the engine. The silence bombarded her senses.

Strine opened her door and the scent of vegetation and a hint of salt water on the breeze filled the car. Night noises—frogs, crickets, dried leaves—chattering on the breeze penetrated the silence.

Paula got out of the car, along with Cutty, who was looking around with an awed expression. They grabbed their bags and turned to the building.

A woman, tall and lean, like Strine, stood at the top of the steps and watched them with gentle, almost motherly eyes.

Paula exchanged looks with Cutty as Strine led the way up the steps. The woman enveloped Strine in a strong embrace and then held her at arm's length. She studied Strine with mild, intelligent eyes and then looked beyond her to Paula and Cutty a few steps down.

"Introduce me to your friends." The woman's voice was sonorous and lilting and wrapped around Paula like a comfortable blanket.

Strine turned around, and Paula and Cutty climbed the last few steps to the top of the veranda.

"This is Archivist Paula Reisling and Chief Cutty Downs," Strine said. "My aunt, Morrigan."

"A pleasure to meet you," Paula said.

"Sorry to barge in on you in the middle of the night like this," Cutty said.

Morrigan cocked her head at Strine. "Strange company you're keeping these days."

"They've turned out to be good company," Strine said.

Morrigan held her hands out. "Welcome to my home. Come in. Let's get you settled in and rested. I have a feeling we have much to talk about."

Understatement seemed to be family trait, Paula mused as she hefted her bag and followed Morrigan and Strine into the lodge.

Chapter 20

CUTTY WOKE UP and frowned at the streaks of bright sun coming in through a wide picture window. She inhaled a scent of wood and lavender and pulled herself up in the rustic bent-wood framed bed, complete with a country comforter and knotted-wood furniture. The room screamed cozy cabin in the woods. Like a peaceful island in the middle of all the drama raging around her. Her Rivendell. Except Celtic women with knowledge of ancient arcane traditions lived here instead of elves. Although at that moment she didn't know which was more intimidating.

For all her motherly gentleness and calm, Morrigan seemed to be made from many threads of mystery woven into her every look and word. Cutty had no problem believing Morrigan was a keeper of the sword, in the same way Strine was believable as the swordbearer. Both had all kinds of mystery enveloping them like an aura.

But not O'Hara . . .

Not O'Hara. Kind of surprising the League didn't feel it. Maybe the magic was only apparent to people who weren't used to it, who were outside the magic circle.

"I'd better get a shower and see what's going on."

A quarter hour later, Cutty stepped into the hallway with five doors total on either side. Morrigan had said the lodge had only twenty-four guest rooms, plus a half-dozen cabins. A great place for a family reunion or a weekend party with a bunch of friends.

She walked to the end of the hallway and the second-floor landing that doubled as a sitting room with a huge stone fireplace. Doors stood on either side of the fireplace. Morrigan had said it used to be the social room for evening dances and concerts and other entertainments.

Her footfalls echoed as she walked down the rustic staircase to the great room—high ceiling, picture windows along the back wall, knots of chairs, table, and sofas huddled around the room. A pool table stood near a bar which probably had been used as the guest check-in counter. A ping pong table was next to one of the picture windows.

A figure, standing at the window, was silhouetted by the bright sunlight. Cutty walked across the shiny flagstone floor to the windows.

She stopped and stared in awe out the window. "Wow."

Paula glanced at her, then returned her attention to the view. "Spectacular isn't it?"

The lodge was perched on a hill with a steep drop to the slate-gray waters of the Juan de Fuca Strait. The choppy water reflected the heavy menacing clouds bunched around the mountains rising out of the water in a dramatic otherworldly way. They looked impenetrable, like something out of a dark fantasy novel.

"You must venture into the mountains of doom . . ." she droned in a deep voice.

Paula glanced at her and chuckled.

"I wonder if Morrigan will let me move in." Cutty watched the clouds drift into each other and slowly spread over the water. "Is that Canada?"

"Yep."

"Cool." Cutty grinned. This adventure was full of new surprises, like seeing her first foreign country.

"Looks like it'll be a good day for learning mysteries," Paula said.

"I bet the storms around here are epic."

Paula picked up a pair of binoculars from a small table in front of the window. "Believe it or not, this part of Washington gets very little rain and is sunny much of the year. Not like the rest of this part of Washington state, which is a rainforest."

Cutty gave her an amused look. "The walking encyclopedia strikes again."

Paula shrugged. "There was a pamphlet about this area in the end table in my room. Probably left there from when this place was a lodge."

"I've got to start becoming a better snoop." Cutty turned at soft footfalls behind her. A young woman who could be Strine's twin walked their way, carrying a tray of what looked and smelled like breakfast.

The woman smiled at them as she put the tray on a low table in front of a nearby sofa.

"Good morning. I'm Brid, Morrigan's eldest daughter, in case you're keeping track." Her eyes sparkled, revealing a buoyant personality. Such a contrast to Strine.

"I'm Paula and this is Cutty."

"She's an archivist for the justice department and I'm a small-town police chief," Cutty said.

"Strange company for Strine to be keeping," Brid said. "But welcome company given the circumstances."

"We hope we can help her and your family," Paula said.

"We hope you can, too. I brought you some breakfast." Brid held her hand out to the tray. "We're informal around here so dig in and let me know if you need more." She turned to Cutty. "The vegetarian one is on the left."

Cutty gave her a surprised look. "Thank you."

"Strine made sure you got properly fed." Brid grinned.

Cutty stared at her, surprised. "I'm in her debt then."

"Be careful"—Brid's eyes sparkled—"she may recruit you to carry her drumsticks on tour."

Cutty laughed. "Well, at least that'd be something to check off my bucket list."

Brid shook her head, amused. "Eat up. We'll be gathering in the parlor in about an hour." She gazed out the window. "It's going to be a good day for a cozy fire." She pointed to a door. "The parlor is through there. Just follow the scent of burning wood and lavender."

"See you in an hour," Paula said as Brid walked toward to the door. She gave Cutty a wry look. "I think this whole adventure is a bucket list buster."

PAULA PULLED THE round-topped door open and blinked as her eyes adjusted to the deep black lit by small, shaded lamps scattered around the largish round chamber and a fire crackling in a stone fireplace with several levels of stone ledges that stretched beyond its boundaries. Earth colored sofas and chairs, cushiony, inviting, and homey formed a tight semi-circle in front of the fireplace separated by low rough-hewed tables.

The warmth chased the chills that had blanketed the main room when the heavy gray clouds had enveloped the lodge, bringing the rain and thunder and lightning halfway through breakfast. Good choice of meeting room.

Morrigan looked up. She was sitting on a cushion on the hearth to one side of the fire. "Come in, come in."

Paula and Cutty stepped into the chamber, letting the door shut behind them. The blackness almost overtook the room. Paula felt like centuries separated the chamber from the rest of the world. Wood, lavender, and a wordless fragrance of age and mystery hung in the air.

Strine sat in a deep chair next to the fire and Morrigan. She gave them a weak smile. "Hi. Hope you slept well." She looked as if she hadn't slept at all.

"Very well, thank you," Cutty said. "And thank you for the vegetarian breakfast."

Strine grinned. "Can't have your stomach growling in the middle of important revelations."

Cutty put her hand to her face. "Thanks."

Morrigan chuckled. "Let me introduce you to my other daughters. This is Birkita, my middle child."

A young woman with fleshier cheeks and a fuller figure than her sisters and cousin nodded to them. "Hi."

"And this is my youngest, Brianna."

Brianna stood and stepped out of the circle through the narrow break between the furniture. She was a younger version of Strine—tall and lean with a strength that was as much a presence as it was physical. She also had the same solemn, calm in her eyes.

"You can get through this way," she said.

"Thanks." Paula squeezed between a sofa and a table. She sat at the far end of the sofa next to Birkita and Brid. Cutty settled in the chair opposite Strine next to the other end of the sofa.

Morrigan pulled a tea kettle from a shelf in front of the fire and poured steaming water into a large porcelain teapot with an intricate Celtic knot painted on it. The pungent odor of tea rose with the steam before she clamped the lid down on the pot.

She looked around the circle, all eyes watching her, waiting.

"So my worst fears have come to pass." She picked up a pair of potholders, lifted the tea pot, and gently moved it in circles. She then lined up seven mugs. "Hmm. Seven. Perfect order. The seventh month, Oak month. The oak, symbolizing protection and magic." She raised her eyes. "Our number is not a coincidence."

She gently shook the pot and poured tea into each mug. She picked up a sweating silver jug with a linen cloth draped over it. She folded back the cloth and poured cream into each mug. Without standing, she used her long body to put the mugs on the long low table within everyone's reach.

"We lift our mugs to our mother goddess, Danu," she said.

Paula lifted her mug, along with the others.

Morrigan passed her hand over her mug.

Paula blinked and caught Cutty's eye. She looked equally mystified. Something changed, like a blanket of air—different, ancient, otherworldly—dropped over them. Even the crackling of the fire seemed to echo from an older time.

Morrigan raised her mug. "To Danu. May she give us the wisdom to set things right." She took a sip.

"To Danu," Paula intoned with the others.

She tasted the tea and was surprised at its deep warmth, like a favorite comforter. She couldn't place the blend, and she had savored many flavors of teas. Whatever it was, she wanted a lifetime supply.

Morrigan put her mug on the table and spread an Afghan over her jeans-clad legs. "Where to begin."

She opened a book with a spine that looked close to a foot thick. Paula raised her chin to get a better look at it. The binding was leather, but relatively new. More surprising, the pages were photographs of very ancient documents.

"Since tradition has been broken, secrets can be spoken." She raised solemn eyes, the deep blue glistening like crystals in the flickering firelight. "Secrets must be spoken to restore tradition."

Strine looked up from staring into her mug. "It's possible?"

Morrigan gave her a motherly reassuring look. "It's possible Danu wouldn't create traditions that could be broken by mere stupidity."

Her daughters and Strine exchanged amused glances.

"The simple fact is, a man can never be a swordbearer and a man can never be a keeper. Even if a man receives the keepership from the League and has access to all the secrets and is in care of the sword. He does not have all the skills to be a keeper."

"But isn't everything in the ancient text?" Brianna looked around as if for support.

Morrigan smiled and took another sip of tea. "Yes."

"But obviously something's missing because he doesn't know how to get the sword back," Brianna said.

"But he said the ancient text explained how, but it didn't work," Brid said.

Strine leaned forward with her elbows on her legs. "He also said the ancient text said the sword must pass to the keeper's next of kin if the swordbearer failed."

Her cousins stared at her in shock.

Brid stared at Strine. "But that would mean—"

"His ever-precious daughter. Yes." Strine lifted her mug in an ironic toast.

"But a swordbearer can't give up the sword unless . . ." Brid's eyes widened as panic chased across her face.

"That's why we hightailed it out of Trinidad," Paula said, softly.

"But the swordbearer can't be killed," Brianna said.

They all turned to Morrigan.

Morrigan put her hand on the book. "When your sister . . . died under mysterious circumstances with only Alys as witness, Aignais and I, following the precepts in the ancient text, discussed the change in the succession." She leaned forward with her elbows on her knees. "The truth is, we'd been . . . suspicious is too strong a word, but at least watchful of Alys since she was a small child. She just didn't have the proper respect for the swordbearer line."

Birkita snorted. "She was always too full of herself. Like she was superior to the rest of us."

"It didn't help that her mother died shortly after she was born and her father did not follow tradition and allow her to be fostered by a women's clan," Morrigan said.

"Her father was the one who put those ideas of superiority in her head," Brid said.

Morrigan nodded. "Most likely. But he is a blood-born son. So rare that only one or two are born a century and it's even rarer they have daughters."

"And the daughters usually have sons," Birkita said. "Removing them from the blood line of the sword and keeper, keeping the female lineage pure."

"Blood-born son?" Cutty asked.

"A male born in the swordbearer line," Morrigan said. "We only take from males the means to make a child, not any of his genetic material. But nothing is completely pure in nature, and a very latent male chromosome surfaces every once in a while."

"Why did O'Hara raise his daughter against tradition?" Paula asked. "Wouldn't his ambitions for her to become swordbearer be better achieved if she grew up with the women and become a part of the inner circle, so to speak?"

Morrigan's eyes twinkled with sad amusement. "Seamus majored in ancient language—actually has a master's degree in it. He made the *fuil gaiscaoch* codices his focus of study."

"The . . . ?" Cutty frowned.

"Basically, a history of the Hibernian League and all the documents maintained by the League from the beginning, including all the stories and lore and references to the ancient text when passages have been cited for various reasons." Morrigan sighed. "As will become clear by the end of this day, what he thinks he was learning was completely wrong, but I couldn't say anything when he challenged Strine's choice of keeper."

Her daughters and Strine exchanged surprised looks.

"Why?" Brianna asked.

"Let me tell the story from the beginning so it all makes sense," Morrigan said.

"I can't believe there was any reason you couldn't stand up to him and stop him." Brianna sat back, her indignation loud and clear.

"I know, daughter," Morrigan said. "This has always been your bane with me. I know you have tried to comprehend, and I've always been grateful for that. I hope today you'll finally understand why I had to do what I did."

Brianna stood and held her long arm over the table. Morrigan took her hand. "I understand that you were positive it was the only choice you had, but I don't understand why tradition allowed a situation where you had to make the choice." She squeezed Morrigan's hand and sat.

Morrigan picked up a thin chain with a medallion hanging from it.

Strine gasped. "You found it?"

"We searched for it several years ago," Morrigan said.

"But how? You're not the keeper . . ." Strine put her hand to her forehead, her expression stricken.

Morrigan laid the medallion on the opened book. "Ah, now I see you're starting to understand."

"All these years I had to deal with him." Strine stared at nothing.

"Is it proper to ask what you're talking about?" Cutty asked.

Morrigan gave her a gentle smile. "This medallion belonged to Aine, Strine's older sister. We found it on the mountainside where she died. Only the keeper has the, let's call it skill to find the traditional belongings of the bloodline."

"So, you're saying you've never stopped being a keeper." Cutty gazed at Strine, who looked close to passing out.

Brid knelt in front of Strine and pulled her into her arms. "Things will be fine from now on."

"I never treated him with respect, but I should have known it was all wrong. I should have rejected him as soon as I was of age." Strine raised her head and gazed at Morrigan. "I never felt the bond that Mother said she felt with you. I just thought it was because I don't naturally respond to males."

"You're a swordbearer without a keeper, and I'm a keeper without a swordbearer. We each have the skills of our positions but we're missing each other's part for the skills to be performed together. But"—Morrigan held up a finger—"our separate skills are enough to restore tradition."

Strine took several deep breaths and put her hands on Brid's shoulders. "Thank you, cousin. I'm feeling better."

Brid nodded and returned to her seat.

Morrigan drained her tea and put the mug rim down on the shelf. "When we suspected Alys may have had something to do with Aine's death, we decided to do what never has been done before." She put her hand on the book. "The ancient text prohibited being copied, except for those pages that were unreadable or damaged beyond repair. But we decided it was fine to photograph the pages, making a copy without physically copying the text."

"Brilliant," Cutty muttered.

Paula glanced at her, and then focused on the book. The ancient text. Right there in front of them.

Strine blinked at the book in wonderment. "I don't believe it."

"But doesn't it say what O'Hara tried to do to restore the sword?" Paula asked.

Morrigan gazed at her with a slow Cheshire Cat smile. "He only sees with what he knows."

Cutty sat up, eyes wide with realization. "It's in code."

Everyone stared at her and then turned to Morrigan.

Morrigan nodded. "Partially, with an added twist." She picked up a palm-sized book with a green binding. She opened it to reveal pages filled with old-fashioned handwriting.

"Sister-talk," Brianna said with a shrug.

Morrigan turned to Cutty and Paula. "One tradition passed down through the centuries is a language spoken among the women in the direct bloodlines. Everyone thinks it was created as a secret women's language to protect the traditions from males and people outside the blood, but those who become keepers learn it actually completes the ancient text."

Brikita frowned. "To protect the ancient text, like in case it falls into the wrong hands or something?"

Morrigan nodded. "Exactly. When O'Hara reads the text, he reads something that makes sense but is not correct. When I read the ancient text, I read the words as sister-talk and that is the true text."

"Cool," Cutty said, looking spellbound.

Paula gave her a curious look and returned her attention to Morrigan. "So, you know what we need to do to fix all this?"

"Yes."

"The next of kin has to take over as swordbearer if the current swordbearer fails?" Paula said.

"No."

"What about the dagger made out of the ingot?" Cutty asked. "That it can kill the swordbearer."

Morrigan chuckled. "Complete nonsense. The ingot exists solely to reveal a false keeper. Instructions involving the ingot are always false. But . . ." She grinned while she turned to a page in the ancient text and put her finger on some words. "'If the keeper is false, the sword cannot complete the mission. The sword will find a way to leave a piece of itself behind.' What O'Hara read is, 'If the sword is damaged, it will not return to the keeper.'"

"That's what he told me," Strine said. "He told me the sword didn't return because it was damaged. The perpetrator had already set the destruction in motion so I sliced the power cord that was hanging high up the wall. The cord split and the sword disappeared. As far as I was concerned the mission had been successfully completed."

"And when he told her the sword had been damaged, you returned to the cave to look for the missing piece," Cutty said. "But I had already found the fragment by then."

"But even if I had found it, O'Hara would have eventually been exposed as a false keeper," Strine said. "Because he doesn't know how to restore the sword."

"Exactly," Morrigan said and put her finger on another passage in the book. "'The sword will appear when the true keeper is restored and the fragment touches the steel of the sword where it was lost.'" She sat back and resettled the Afghan in her lap.

Paula exchanged stunned looks with everyone else.

"How . . . ?" Cutty blinked around as if unsure about breaking the deep silence. "How is the keeper restored?"

Morrigan shrugged. "All I have to do is touch the sword." She rested her eyes on Paula.

Paula straightened, and the others turned to her. She slipped her hand into her jacket pocket and pulled out a bundle of soft leather.

Strine stared at it. "You have it with you?"

Paula gave her an apologetic smile. "I thought it best you didn't know so you wouldn't worry about it."

Strine let out an unsteady breath. "Can I . . . ?"

Paula stood, as did Strine. Paula handed it to her over the low table past Strine's cousins.

Strine gazed at the cloth cradled in her hands. "I've only held the sword once and for only a few seconds, yet it lives within me with every breath I take, with every beat of my heart." She looked up, tears streaking down her cheeks. "My soul has been shattered since that day. As if a part of me was lost with the sword."

She carefully pulled back the cloth and stared at the fragment nestled in the soft leather. Without touching it, she held it out to Morrigan.

Morrigan closed the ancient text. "Put it on the book."

Strine laid the cloth on the book. The fragment nestled on top of it, multi-colors gleaming in the firelight.

Morrigan gazed at the fragment with sad eyes. "What has that man done to you? Done to our traditions? My precious, noble sword." She hovered her fingers over the fragment, then lowered them to rest on the steel.

Paula didn't know what to expect and was a little disappointed. Not even a little spark or wisp of vapor.

Morrigan lifted her fingers and glanced around with an enigmatic, yet satisfied look. She held her hand out to Strine.

Strine blinked at it for a moment, then grasped it. Her eyes widened, and she drew in a deep breath, her expression stunned, but with a look of wonder, rather than dismay.

"I've never felt this before," she said in a voice thick with emotion.

"This is what it feels like to be connected to a keeper," Morrigan said.

Strine shook her head, still looking amazed.

"But . . ." Cutty glanced around sheepishly.

Everyone turned to her.

"How did Strine and the sword know to, uh, go into action?"

Strine frowned at her then turned to Morrigan.

Morrigan shook her head. "The way the sword and the swordbearer always knows. I am only the keeper of the sword. I have no control over it or the swordbearer."

"So it broke because it wasn't properly cared for?" Cutty asked.

"Exactly," Morrigan said. "It needs to be tended to in specific ways that can only be read in the text by a true keeper."

"The true keeper has been restored," Brianna said. "How do we get the sword back?"

"That fragment has to touch the ingot where the sword was lost," Brid said.

"Which O'Hara has conveniently taken from the inaccessible place it's kept," Paula said.

Morrigan grinned and rewrapped the fragment and slipped it into her pocket. She opened the ancient text, flipped through several pages, and stopped. "The ancient texts made sure the false keeper does just that. This is what O'Hara read. 'To restore the sword, the swordbearer must be destroyed with the steel of the blade and be replaced by the next of the sister-blood.'"

"So, he really thinks that dagger can kill Strine," Brikita said.

"Yes, and we can use that to lure him and Alys back to the scene of the crime," Paula said.

Morrigan straightened and looked around. "It looks like we're taking a road trip."

Chapter 21

CUTTY SUCKED IN a breath of the mix of fall foliage and salt water. Heaven. Nothing less. She had never thought that she could find anything to entice her away from Southern Illinois, but the Pacific Northwest had really touched something deep inside her.

She went to the railing of the back veranda and stared out at the mountains across the strait, foreboding and inviting. What she would give to be able to explore them, explore a whole new country, or float on a boat in that sparkling strait that wound inland all the way to Seattle.

Something wild and untamed, like clans of swordbearers and keepers. Not of this world. Not of this time. Yet as natural as the land.

She glanced back at footfalls behind her.

Paula walked up to the railing and gazed at the clear sky. "Kind of grows on you, doesn't it."

"It's almost magical," Cutty asked.

Paula grinned as she gazed at the Canadian shoreline. "It is magical. The whole Pacific Northwest coast is."

Cutty watched a pair of squirrels scamper up and down a thick-trunked tree. "I definitely want to explore it."

"Well"—Paula rocked on her heels with her hands stuffed into her khakis—"I happen to know a guide who works for cheap . . . with the right client."

Cutty gave her an amused look. "Right client, huh?"

"Yeah." Paula shrugged, smile tugging at her lips. "The kind of client who loves the outdoors"—she looked Cutty up and down—"already has the clothing"—she gazed up at the cloudless sky—"be fun to share a tent with."

Cutty raised an eyebrow. "That guide sounds awfully forward."

Paula studied her boots. "Only if the client isn't the right one."

Cutty nodded, pretending to ponder the offer, while her insides were shaking with a happy laugh. Who would have thought a geeky wardrobe-challenged archivist would be her type, but she had felt the connection the moment they met.

"Well." Cutty put her hands behind her back and walked around Paula, making her turn away from the balcony. "The client has to also make sure the guide is the right one."

Paula raised an eyebrow. "Besides being cheap?"

Cutty stepped forward, pulled Paula to her, and kissed her.

Paula blinked at her, looking a bit owlish through her glasses. "Did I pass the test?"

Cutty waggled her head. "Preliminary test looks promising."

"Promising, huh?" Paula leaned in and captured Cutty's lips in a longer, pleasantly persuasive kiss.

"Very promising." Cutty cleared her throat. "But it never hurts to continue the testing."

Paula laughed. "I like the way you think."

PAULA FELT A wave of déjà vu as she stepped off the plane at the Eureka-Arcata airport. She never thought she'd travel this way again before her retirement years—certainly not twice in a week. The mid-morning fog was still thick and gray. The moist chill soaked through her jacket as she walked into the terminal and past the security area to the waiting area.

She scanned the small crowd of people. Chris was being fashionably late as usual. She shouldered her backpack—glad she had sent her duffel on with Cutty.

"Damn, girl."

Paula spun around. A diminutive young woman stood there with her hands on her hips. Chris had filled out a bit, and her hair was a more respectable shoulder-length, befitting an ecology professor, but her eyes still had the same I'm-game-for-anything twinkle in them.

Paula put her hands on her hips. "What?"

Chris laughed and pulled Paula into a hug. "Didn't think I'd get a chance to actually see you this trip."

"I was just thinking the same thing," Paula said.

"Well, I'm not complaining," Chris said as they walked to the door. "I'm just happy I get to do something fun and different on my Sunday."

"Different." Paula pushed through the door and stared at the bank of fog sitting over the shore in the distance. "Fun. I hope so."

Chris led the way to the almost-empty parking lot. "So, you're stalking someone who's stalking someone else?"

Paula grinned as they stopped next to a Chevy Bolt. Not surprising, given Chris's complaints about using gas as fuel when they were in college. She tossed her pack into the back and climbed in.

Chris slip into the driver's side.

"I'm actually here to help the stalker find who he's stalking because he's carelessly lost her but doesn't know it yet," Paula said.

Chris gave her an amused look. "Even your research is twisted."

Paula shrugged. "I *am* the Director of the Repository of Unusual Unsolvable Crimes."

Chris pulled to the parking lot exit. "Trinidad?"

"Yep."

"There's breakfast for you in the bag." Chris nodded at the dashboard in front of Paula, then eased onto the road.

"Ah, thank you." Paula grabbed the bag and opened it. She pulled out the Styrofoam container. The aromas were heavenly. She lifted the lid and grinned at pancakes with potatoes on the side.

"It's a pancake sandwich from Crosswinds," Chris said. "Multi-grain pancakes. Syrup should be in the bag with a fork. Bacon, two eggs, and home-style potatoes. Coffee is in the cup next to you."

Paula poured the syrup over the pancakes and sunk her fork through the stack. "All this traveling makes me famished."

Chris laughed. "Sitting still reading a book makes you famished. It's that bird metabolism you have."

"There's just so much good food out there," Paula said between chews.

"And what about this intriguing police chief you've been sharing brain cells with?" Chris rolled off the off-ramp onto 101 into McKinleyville's version of a morning rush hour.

Paula put down her fork. "We seem to make a good pair at solving mysteries."

"Obviously." Chris glanced at her. "And?"

Paula shrugged and picked up her fork. "We've decided to get to know each other better."

"Ah, hah." Chris grinned.

Paula could only shake her head and dig into her pancakes. She was lucky that Chris wasn't the type who wanted to know everything. She wasn't sure what more to say, except she really like Cutty and did not want the end of this case to be the end of everything between them.

They passed the last exit to McKinleyville. "When we get to Trinidad, pull into Murphy's so we can find the stalkers."

"Is being director of an archives everything you thought it would be?" Chris asked.

"Better," Paula said. "I get to be my own boss and research mysteries that the FBI deem unsolvable."

"What makes them unsolvable?"

Paula swallowed a mouthful of egg. "Many factors."

"They're like cold cases?" Chris glanced at her.

"Uh, no." Paula took a sip of coffee. "There's an actual division for those."

Chris flashed her a curious look. "And yours are different how?"

"Well . . ." Paula inwardly sighed. How to explain the indescribable? "Cold cases go cold because there just isn't enough evidence to find or prove a perpetrator. Sometimes there are suspects—strong suspects—but all the evidence is circumstantial."

"Okay." Chris drew out the word.

"The cases that are put in the archives are"—Paula tried to find the right words—"complete mysteries. There isn't any evidence at all. It's like the crime was committed in a vacuum."

Chris frowned. "But there was enough evidence to know a crime was committed."

"Yes," Paula said. "Most of the crimes are murder."

"Is this case murder?"

"Yep." Paula popped the last mouthful of pancake into her mouth.

"And you're trying to find the murderer?"

Paula swallowed and gave Chris a wry look. "Nope."

Chris glanced at her . . . twice. "Huh?"

"We've found the murderer," Paula said. "Now we're trying to keep her alive and restore her livelihood."

Chris glanced at her with a confused frown. "Say what?"

"I promise to tell you the whole story when we have an ending for it," Paula said.

Chris scrunched her brow for a few seconds. "Okay. As long as I have a cool cameo in the story."

Paula laughed. "Guaranteed." She shook her head in amusement. "Guaranteed."

Chapter 22

CUTTY TRIED TO keep from grinning as Jen nipped at her heels all the way down the corridor to her office. Jen was also making tiny, excited noises.

Cutty went through her doorway and stepped aside to let Jen scurry in. Jen pounced on her favorite chair like a puppy after a long walk. Cutty shook her head and went to her desk and picked up the stack of mail in the wire inbox.

"Well?" Jen was probably doing some internal damage to herself, holding in her excitement and curiosity.

Cutty calmly sorted through the stack of mail and put it back into the inbox. "Well?"

Jen ran her hands through her hair. "Stop torturing me."

Cutty laughed and leaned back against her desk with her arms crossed. "What if I were to tell you it's all hush-hush top-secret stuff and I can't say anything about it?"

Jen grabbed her hair. "Agghh!"

Cutty grinned and sat in the chair next to Jen's. "Yes, Strine of The Black Warriors is here in Lipping Creek, resting in Mrs. Livesay's B&B." She held up her hand. "I can't tell you why."

"Are you still working on that FBI case?" Jen looked genuinely bewildered.

"Yes," Cutty said.

"And Strine has something to do with it?"

Cutty sighed. "Would you be willing to just go along with it right now if I promise to tell you the whole story when this mission is over."

Jen gazed at her, and Cutty could almost see the million answers whirling through her mind. "Do I have a choice?"

"That would be a no." Cutty settled back as she let the fact that she was actually home in her own office after literally running all over the country sink in. "I do have a favor to ask. The cave needs a little preparation for our visitors."

Jen grinned. "Whatever you need, boss."

"Excellent."

Jen gave a head a shake. "So that's really Strine?"

Cutty laughed. "I warned her that you're The Black Warriors' biggest fan, so she'll cut you some slack, but get it out of your system fast because I'm going to need you to help keep her presence here low key."

"I get to be her bodyguard?" Jen squeaked.

"Local escort," Cutty said. "The women with her are her aunt, Morrigan, and cousin, Brianna."

"Wow," Jen said.

"No badgering them about Strine." Cutty gave her a knowing look.

"I can't fall to my knees and kiss Strine's feet?" Jen gave her a feigned puppy dog look.

Cutty rolled her eyes. "It'll be good for you to be around her, I think. Just to learn that she's an ordinary person with a rather flashy job."

CHRIS PARKED CLOSE to the casino door, not much business in the middle of the day.

Strine had hinted that Alys got bored easily and liked to play the slots. That explained her presence at the casino two nights earlier.

The sheriff had reported that only O'Hara was outside Stine's house. So the first logical place to look for Alys was the casino.

They climbed out of the car and Chris looked up at the multi-Indian lodge inspired building.

"Ever been here?" Paula asked.

Chris shook her head. "I'm not a casino type person."

"Hold your breath," Paula said. "The place reeks of smoke."

"Lovely." Chris grinned but braced her shoulders. "The things I do for fun."

Paula laughed as she slipped on her Buddy Holly glasses and mussed up her hair. She led the way up the steep drive to the bank of glass doors, which opened automatically and a tear-inducing stale and smokey wall pushed out into the brisk air.

Chris turned away for a few moments then followed Paula through the doorway. The incessant slots pinging and dinging made the place seem much busier than the couple of dozen people perched on stools, feeding the token eating beasts.

"Let's check the slots," Paula said.

They started along the side of the slot area and pretended to be looking for a machine to play on.

"I can't remember what it's called but I know what it looks like," Paula said.

"Very helpful," Chris said as they got to the end of the row.

Paula squinted at an alcove containing a few slots and two very cantankerous looking people.

Alys was sitting on a stool, attacking the buttons on the machine like they were her greatest enemy. She also seemed to be voicing some discontentment.

Paula grinned. "We've made contact."

Chris looked into the alcove. "Wow. I wouldn't want to cross her."

"From what I hear, she was born with a winning combination of entitlement and nastiness." Paula led the way to the wall next to the alcove, covered with coming attractions posters and thankfully free of slots.

Paula nodded to Chris who took out her phone and punched in a number. Darth Vadar's theme filled the air.

Paula pulled out her phone. "Paula here. I'm looking for them now. I heard that the daughter likes to gamble, so I'm scouting the casino. Saw their rental car in the parking lot."

Chris smirked as she disconnected her phone.

"Yeah," Paula said into the phone. "Cutty is driving her to the Sacramento airport . . . Yeah, in case they have someone watching the airport here."

Paula paused and looked in the direction of the alcove. Alys had stopped talking and the machine's frantic noise was calmer. She lifted her chin in the direction of the row of slots with a view of the alcove.

Chris grinned and went to a slot machine in the middle of the row with a good view of Alys.

"They're catching a red eye to St. Louis. Someone will pick them up to take them the rest of the way." Paula watched Chris, who pretended to read the slot instructions as she flicked curious glances at Alys.

"They have to return to the cave to get the sword back," Paula said in a rather impatient voice. "No really. That's what Strine said . . . Yes . . . I don't understand it either but what else can we do?"

Chris's eyes widened and then relaxed a bit.

Paula knew she had to finish the phone call and get out of sight. "I've got to go. I'll keep you posted. Yeah. Bye."

She pocketed the phone and turned to walk away from the alcove to the bar entrance. She paused, then walked in and sat at a table.

Chris walked in a few minutes later and almost trotted to the table, unable to stop her grin.

"Oh, that was classic," she said as she clasped her hands together on the tabletop. "They were petrified that you were going to find them, so they moved to the slots facing the far wall. When you stopped talking, they waited a few minutes and peeked around the corner. When they saw you were gone, they made a beeline for the door."

"Another successful caper," Paula said.

"That you're going to tell me all about." Chris raised a pointed eyebrow.

"Hopefully, sooner rather than later . . . if all goes to plan."

Chapter 23

THE TALL, LEAN, not to mention formidable Cearnaigh women strode through the sparse trees with a grace and confidence that Cutty knew came from the deep sister spirit they possessed. Even in jeans tucked into leather boots and thick Shetland sweaters, they looked like warriors from another time.

Strine knew the way, but it was Morrigan who was a step ahead of her and Brianna. Cutty and Paula and Jen could only follow. The resolution to this whole unbelievable adventure was in the hands of these women.

Normally, Cutty would have been savoring such a sunny winter day with the cold just touching her cheeks, but she couldn't ignore breakfast doing flip-flops in her stomach. Did Morrigan really know what she was doing? So many things could go wrong fast between bladed weapons and guns in a very small dark space.

She glanced at Paula, who seemed to be studying the landscape. "We need to go a little north so we'll be shielded by a small outcropping."

Morrigan glanced back, nodded, and turned toward a denser clump of trees.

"Why do I feel she's led armies on horseback in several former lives?" Cutty muttered.

"Nothing surprises me anymore," Paula muttered back.

They entered a copse of tall spindly birch trees edged by a finger of a rocky outcropping parallel to the looming Gardner bluff.

"The cave is over there." Cutty pointed to the south. Several people-sized boulders stood in front of the bluff, partially hiding the deeper color from the cave. "From where they parked, they take a trail for about two miles to the base of the bluff and then simply follow it for about a half mile."

Paula shaded her eyes as she looked in the direction O'Hara and company would be coming from. "How soon will they be here?"

"Probably another fifteen minutes, if they're good walkers," Cutty said.

"Seamus will be pushing it. He's so close to getting what he's wanted all these years." Morrigan turned to Strine and Brianna and put a hand on their shoulders. "It's time. We're going into unknown territory here. All we can do is trust the ancient text."

Strine and Brianna nodded with determined expressions.

"We won't fail," Strine said. "We cannot fail."

Morrigan released Strine's and Brianna's shoulders and turned. "And it helps to have backup."

"Glad to be here to help," Cutty said. "But I'd really appreciate it, if we just get to watch."

Morrigan laughed. "We'll try to oblige."

Paula spun around and stared at the bluff. "I think I hear voices."

"Voices tend to echo off the shelter bluffs," Cutty said.

Strine straightened. "I guess it's showtime."

Cutty sucked in a breath as the reality of what they were about to attempt sank in. "Good luck."

"I hope to get a chance to see the sword that has caused all this mess before it disappears," Paula said.

Morrigan cocked her head with an enigmatic sparkle in her eyes. "We're traveling a new path in the history of Blood Hero. I expect there will be some surprises."

Cutty exchanged glances with Paula. "Good surprises, I hope."

"Good or not, I'm sure they'll be memorable," Brianna said. "The air is filled with wild magic."

Jen's eyes widened and Brianna ghosted her a wink. Cutty suspected it wasn't just because of the wild magic. Jen had taken on the job of keeping Brianna entertained. Brianna had even helped her with the cave preparations.

The voices were louder accompanied by the crunch of leaves.

"I see them," Paula said, as she stepped behind the outcropping with Cutty and Jen.

"Now it's really showtime." Morrigan straightened and walked out of the copse of trees followed by Strine and Brianna.

The voices and crunching stopped. Cutty peeked around a boulder. O'Hara was motioning Alys into a shelter bluff. They watched as the trio of Cearnaigh women stride to the cave and disappear inside it.

"That was easy." Paula leaned in behind her to see around the boulder.

"I really hope they know what they're doing." Cutty pushed down her apprehension. It was going to work, one way or another.

"I don't know about you"—Paula stepped back behind the rocks—"but I felt that wild magic coming off of them."

Cutty cocked her head at her. "I was kind of hoping that's what I felt."

"They're on the move," Jen said in a low voice.

They all leaned as far as they could around the boulders to watch O'Hara and Alys strutting through the leaves as if they owned the world.

"Looks like they left the worthless husband with the car," Paula said.

O'Hara and Alys stopped in front of the cave opening.

"Where are they?" Alys asked.

"Well, they certainly know where you are," Cutty muttered.

Jen snorted a laugh.

Cutty nodded to where the outcropping turned toward the bluff north of the cave. "Let's skirt around that way, so they don't see us."

Paula took a crunching step. "Oops."

"Gotta teach you the art of walking in the woods." Cutty grinned as she passed Paula with just a whisper from her boots.

"Looking forward to it." Paula carefully put each foot down as she followed Cutty and Jen to a boulder that stood sentinel near the stream and about ten feet from the bluff.

O'Hara stepped into the cave, followed by an eager-looking Alys.

"Ready?" Cutty glanced at Jen and then hopped across the dry creek bed into a shelter cave next to the cave opening with Jen behind her.

They followed the wall of the shelter cave, their footfalls soft on the sandy ground, and put themselves next to the cave entrance.

"It's too dark," Alys said. "Why didn't you bring a flashlight?"

Cutty heard O'Hara's impatient sigh. "I've got one on my phone." A very weak light flickered around in the dark.

"That helps." Alys's voice was both sarcastic and contemptuous.

Cutty exchanged looks with Jen. O'Hara really raised a piece of work.

"Anyway, where are they?" Alys asked.

"I think that dark area over there is more of the cave," O'Hara said.

Cutty peeked into the cave. O'Hara and Alys were facing the entrance to the inner chamber on the opposite side. O'Hara aimed his phone flashlight into the dark area. Alys's dagger glinted in the weak light as she held it in front of her. They stepped forward together and paused in the dark spot.

Cutty reached around the opening of the cave and pushed a button. The dark area filled with blinding light. She and Jen stepped as quietly as possible across the cave to stand behind O'Hara and Alys, who were frozen in shock.

Cutty looked back at the cave entrance where Paula was peeking in and aiming her camera at the scene. She gave her a thumbs up and returned her attention to the amazing scene inside the side chamber.

Morrigan and Brianna flanked Strine against the opposite wall of the inner cave, looking both relaxed and alert, with that you-don't-scare-me swagger Cutty would love to possess even a fraction.

Alys unfroze first and glared at Strine. "It's my time!" She lifted the dagger.

Morrigan and Brianna lifted their arms in front of them and as they brought their hands together long silver swords materialized in time for their fingers to wrap around the hilts.

"One little known part of the swordkeeper's duty is to also be the keeper of the swordbearer when the situation arises." Morrigan nodded to Brianna and they brought their swords down on the dagger.

"Ahh," Alys cried as she dropped the dagger and held her hand under her arm as if it had been burned.

"I'm the keeper of the sword," O'Hara said as he knelt, bent forward, and reached for the dagger.

Morrigan put the tip of her sword on the back of his neck. "Don't think I don't have the guts to do it."

O'Hara let out a frustrated growl as he pulled his hand back.

Strine held up the fragment, dropped to her knees, and touched it to the dagger. Both dissolved in a glowing green mist that grew so thick it obscured the ground. Something long and silver glinted beneath the mist and Alys lunged forward.

"Not so fast," Cutty said as she grasped Alys by the shoulders and jerked her back.

Strine reached into the mist and lifted a long silver sword, with intricate Celtic markings almost dancing on the blade, and a hilt of steel twisted in the shape of a dragon.

Jen grabbed O'Hara and yanked him to his feet.

The mist cleared, leaving a block of steel, which Morrigan swept up and dropped into a pouch hanging from her belt. Strine stood and she and her keeper and her cousin held the swords out in front of them.

Cutty and Jen handcuffed O'Hara and Alys as they stared at the sword with shocked expressions.

"The sword and the swordbearer are safe," Morrigan said.

She and Brianna turned and touched their blades to Strine's. The swords dissolved in a shimmering glow from their hands.

Morrigan faced O'Hara, walked up to him, and lifted his chin with a finger so he had to look her in the eyes. "You see, you were never the keeper of the sword. You were never allowed to even see the sword."

O'Hara struggled against Jen's hold on his arms. "That's because the ancient text said . . ."

"The ancient text was written to reveal and misdirect a false keeper," Morrigan said. "And it did its job well, because here we are . . . order restored."

"How—?"

"I don't need to explain anything to you." Morrigan cocked her head. "I've already let the League know your branch of the clan has been cast out from our blood line. You should be receiving the official banishment from the League from them."

O'Hara straightened. "I'll tell them how this was all a plot against me because I'm male. I'm well-respected—"

"I won't miss your arrogant blustering." Morrigan grinned as Cutty and Jan pulled O'Hara and Alys into the outer cave.

Paula backed out of the way as she lowered her camera. "That was the coolest thing I've ever witnessed."

Cutty grinned as she shoved Alys out the cave. "You and me both."

NEVER IN A million years would Cutty have dreamed she'd be introducing the wonders of White Bluff State Park to a genuine rock star and members of her equally fascinating family. She was both surprised and not surprised that they wanted to see the park. And, of course, Paula was eager to see this place that Cutty probably talked way too much about in Virginia.

Fortunately, it was a beautiful cool day, and she loved the bare silhouette of the trees against the blue sky. Cutty steered them away from the more popular trails. Late afternoons brought out people, even on winter days if the sun was shining.

"This is my favorite hollow," she said as they ambled down a trail that followed a rocky creek with water flowing beneath thin sheets of cracked ice. Walls of white stone steadily rose on either side of the creek as the hollow deepened and narrowed.

Strine looked up and around. "The temperature is cooler."

"It's really nice in the summer when it's a hundred-plus degrees and considerably cooler down here." Cutty ran her hands over a patch of ferns.

"I can see why you love it here," Morrigan said.

"The whole national forest is like this." Cutty walked ahead as the trail narrowed between the rock wall and the creek. "But since I had a chance to see other parts of this country, I now want to get out and explore." She paused as they rounded a curve and faced a frozen waterfall with water trickling beneath the ice where the walls met in a dramatic rise to the top of the bluff. "This place will always be home, but I realized I can hold it in here"—she tapped her chest—"and still be happily away." She glanced at a grinning Paula.

Morrigan ran her hand over the rocky wall. "There is an abundance of wild magic here. So refreshing and rare. Maybe that's why Danu led us to this place to restore our traditions."

"I like that," Cutty said, delighted by the idea. "There's something that's been bothering me, though. There was only one set of footprints in the cave. But Strine stood in the cave when she stabbed him and walked to the wall to cut the power cord."

Paula, along with Strine and Briana, turned to Morrigan, who gifted them with a motherly smile.

"That's simple," she said. "It wouldn't do to do the deed and disappear and leave something behind. When the swordbearer vanishes, all traces of her ever being there goes with her."

Four Months Later

CUTTY COULDN'T STAND being at her desk with the birds twittering as they nested in the trees outside her windows. The bench in front was much better. The week of spring break always brought a constant stream of visitors to the state park every day, as the warm weather burst through the lingering damp cold of winter. The line in front of Marge's was out the door and the bicyclists skirted alongside the stream of cars on their way to the park entrance.

A normal, beautiful spring day in Southern Illinois, yet she didn't feel the sparkle, the magic she had always felt on days like today. Her world had been expanded too much for her to be contained in this small piece of paradise.

Her phone buzzed. She pulled it out of her pocket and smiled at the name as she accepted the call and put it to her ear. "Greetings, fair archivist."

Paula laughed. 'Only half right."

Cutty shrugged. "It sounded good."

"Well, we just got a visit from none other than Marion Smythe," Paula said. "She was so excited about our case that she came in person to get all the details."

"Wow." Cutty frowned. "Is that a good thing?"

"Well, it gave her an idea," Paula said.

"Is *that* a good thing?"

"She wants to expand the scope of the Archives."

"Expand?" As much as Cutty enjoyed bantering with Paula, she was ready for her to get the point.

"Add a new department." Cutty could hear Paula's grin in her voice. "A crime solving department, as in solving unusual, unsolvable crimes."

Cutty pushed down a trickle of excitement. "You mean she wants you to keep trying to solve these crimes?"

"She wants us to keep trying to solve them." Paula laughed. "She wants you to be the head of the unsolvable crimes unit."

"What?" Cutty said too loudly and waved her apology to several people walking by.

Paula cleared her throat. "I'm making a job offer."

Cutty sat back and calmed her racing mind. "A job offer, huh?"

"Yes," Paula said. "One with great benefits."

"Oh, I don't know"—Cutty grinned at a town cat investigating something on the sidewalk—"I've got some pretty good benefits now."

"Well, I admit being surrounded by a national forest and having a state park in your backyard is a pretty good job perk . . ."

Cutty pictured Paula gazing innocently up at the ceiling. "And a nice bench to sit on to people watch."

"Yep, there's that," Paula said. "But do you have your own gourmet cook, who loves the challenge of cooking vegetarian meals?"

"That would be a no."

"Or a free place to live?"

Cutty looked at her phone and put it back to her ear. "You don't pay any rent? Seriously?"

"That's why we all live here. No one said we couldn't, and no one seems to mind. Marion certainly doesn't have a problem with it."

"Wow." Cutty was having a tough time playing hard to get. "Any other benefits?"

"You know the salary will be more than you're making now," Paula said. "Marion is very generous when she loves an idea."

"Humm." Cutty gazed up at the cloudless sky. "That all sounds pretty good . . ."

"There's one more benefit, more like a perk actually . . . We won't have to compare calendars to coordinate visits anymore."

"Oh yeah. Coordinating calendars is such an arduous task—"

"The best perk is, I'll be close enough to put you in choke hold when you're too stubborn to say yes," Paula said, sounding as if she was holding back a chuckle.

Cutty's shoulder shook from keeping in a laugh. "I'd like to see you try . . . put me in a choke hold that is."

"Well, one of my perks is you trying to teach me to do a choke hold first."

Cutty was grinning so hard it almost hurt. "That sounds like it could be fun."

"How about April first as the start date," Paula said. "Seems appropriate."

"Too perfect." Cutty gazed at the house on the hill above the shops across the way. Her grandfather would not only understand, he'd put her in a choke hold himself if she didn't say yes. "You know how you said you have the dream job you would have dreamed of having if you knew it had existed?"

"Yeah," Paula drew out in a puzzled voice.

"I think solving unusual unsolvable crimes sounds like my dream job."

She heard a muffled "She said yes" and a whooping and hollering in the background.

Yep. It was time to stop sitting on this bench and daydreaming and start seeing what else the world had to throw at her.

T.J. Mindancer may be a figment of someone's imagination or just someone who likes to imagine she's a figment while she creates worlds for her characters to inhabit. She has spent her life working with books as an academic librarian and as an editor for two publishing companies and has had some of her scribbled words published under a couple of pen names—at least one, not a figment. Her work includes the *Tales of Emoria* series of books and shorter tales set in the Emoria world.

In her spare time she likes to see what she can do with pencils, paints, and an assortment of surfaces; plays with sounds and music (she even has a couple of degrees in that); and lives in a tiny house that has a dragon infestation. Fortunately, the dragons are pretty friendly and like her wildly eclectic taste in music and television shows. They even tolerate the sword she keeps by the door.

www.ingramcontent.com/pod-product-compliance
Lightning Source LLC
Chambersburg PA
CBHW050741250626
47155CB00005B/1876